Y0-DWM-753

# Thin Ice

# Books by Marc Talbert

*Dead Birds Singing*
*Thin Ice*

# Thin Ice

## Marc Talbert

AN AUTHORS GUILD BACKINPRINT.COM EDITION

*Thin Ice*

AN AUTHORS GUILD BACKINPRINT.COM EDITION

Published by iUniverse.com, Inc.

For information address:
iUniverse.com, Inc.
5220 S 16th, Ste. 200
Lincoln, NE 68512
www.iuniverse.com

Originally published by Little Brown & Co.

ISBN: 0-595-20019-2

Printed in the United States of America

*For Mary and Will Talbert*
*who coauthored me*
*and*
*Moo Thorpe*
*who reads me like a book*

# Chapter 1

Click.

Martin winced and scrunched his eyes to shut out the flash of the bedroom light. He didn't want to get up.

Click. Click.

He growled softly, frowned so hard his eyebrows covered his eyes, and yanked his covers over his head.

Clickclickclickclickclickclickclick. Click.

His breath, trapped under the covers, was hot and sticky and smelled like sour milk. Sweat popped out on his skin. His pajamas clung in tight places.

I have the world's dumbest sister, Martin fumed. He pictured her standing by the light switch, flicking it on and off and on and off as fast as she could. In his mind he saw her with a crazy "show-'em-your-teeth-all-the-way-back-to-your-tonsils" smile and getting ready to start flicking the switch again.

The covers crept down his neck. He clutched at them but they slipped through his fingers before he could grab tight. The room's chill hit the sweaty gap between his pajama bottoms and top. Goose bumps rippled up and down his back.

"That does it!" Martin sputtered, scrambling onto his knees. Punching his fists into the mattress, he twirled around and saw his sister standing at the foot of his bed. She was dressed for school, holding his blanket in her hand and smiling.

"What's so funny?" Martin glowered.

His sister blinked, wide-eyed, and giggled. "You!" she snickered.

Martin quickly looked down to see if he was poking out of his pajamas. Relieved, he looked back up at his sister. "Ha! Ha!" Martin barked. He bounced on his knees, kicked his legs out straight, swung them over the side of the bed, and stamped his feet on the floor.

Martin lunged and Franny dropped the blanket and scurried out of the room. He raced after her, out the door, down the hall, through the living room, feet pounding on wood and carpeting. He burst into the kitchen and skidded to a halt, his bare feet squeaking on the linoleum.

Franny sat at the kitchen table, smiling, trying to breathe casually through her nose. But she snorted softly as her chest strained in and out. In front of her, arranged as neatly as a table setting, were a syringe, an alcohol wipe, and a little bottle of insulin.

"I need . . . thirty units," she said breathlessly. "I've already tested . . . my pee."

"Why do you do this to me?" Martin groaned,

throwing his arms up in the air and letting them flop to his sides. Every morning for the past few months he and Franny had gone through the same routine. She got him out of bed so he could give her an insulin shot. The first week or so Martin thought it was fun — all the different ways she'd get him up. But, like an old joke told again and again, it was no longer funny. Sometimes, like today, he didn't want to wake up. And some mornings he didn't want to handle needles.

Franny studied him, tilting her head, as if he were an especially strange-looking fish in an aquarium. "Martin," she said, "you *happen* to give the *best* shots in the *world.*"

"Like hell I do," Martin said. Until last year you only let Dad give you shots, he thought. Now that Dad is gone, I have to. Too bad Mom doesn't like needles, he grumbled to himself.

"There's no need for you to swear," Franny said, drawing her back straight and tall.

"Yeah, yeah, yeah," Martin mumbled. He reached for the little bottle of insulin and shook it gently. Someday I'll have enough money to go up to Alaska and spit in Dad's eye, he thought. Or at least tell him what I think of him.

Martin reached for the syringe, which had a hard plastic cover over the needle. He popped off the cover. Giving his sister her insulin shots was worse than a paper route. Martin sighed. They had to be given at the same time every morning. If her shot was late, Franny felt sick or, if it was even later, she sometimes passed out. Martin never got to sleep late anymore or get up when he wanted. Once he'd even given Franny her shot when *he* was sick in bed.

"How was your pee?" he asked, sitting down next to Franny. Franny had to test her pee every morning to see if it had any sugar in it. Sugar meant she wasn't getting enough insulin or that she was eating too many sweets.

"Warm and smelly," Franny said, with a straight face.

"You know what I mean," Martin said. *Doesn't she ever get tired of that joke?* "Any sugar?"

"Nope."

Martin knew she was lying by the way her nostrils pinched together. He also knew that she'd eaten a birthday treat at school yesterday — a big brownie. Franny had a horrible sweet tooth. Even though she wasn't supposed to, she always helped herself to treats when somebody had a birthday. And it always showed the next day in her pee — lots of sugar.

"Sure, Sweet Pea," Martin said, sticking the needle in the bottle's rubber top, tipping the bottle upside down, and drawing out the same amount as usual. Holding the syringe pointed up, he flicked a bubble toward the needle and squeezed it out. "Where did I stick you yesterday?"

"My left leg."

"OK. Today I stick the right leg." Martin brandished the needle in the air, waving it back and forth. He screwed his face into a snarl, crossed his eyes, and leaned forward, breathing heavily into her face. In a gruff, slurred voice he said, "Jus' show me some fle-

esh and I'll sssstick this little sssstinger in so far tha'
it'll squirt ins-s-sulin out the other ssssside!"

"Mar-tin," Franny sighed. She tried to look non-
chalant, but she pressed her lips together and looked
away.

"OK, OK." Martin relaxed his face and eyes.
Quickly, without thinking, Martin pushed back the
hem of Franny's dress, wiped a patch of skin with the
alcohol pad, bunched up the skin, stuck in the needle,
checked for blood, and pushed in the plunger.

"When the hell are you going to learn to do this
for yourself?" he asked, taking the needle out.

"When you let me practice on you," Franny said.
Martin stood up and turned away from her. "Besides,"
Franny's voice faded as he walked away, toward their
bedroom, "someday they'll have a cure for diabetes
and I won't need shots."

Fat chance she'll ever poke her needles into me,
Martin thought. I'd end up looking like the tomato-
shaped pincushion that Mom has in her sewing basket.
Besides, by the time they find a cure for diabetes we'll
all have something else — like cancer.

Martin stopped in the doorway and stared into
the bedroom that he shared with his sister.

"Sheesh," he muttered. "What a pit. She acts like
I don't even live here." He picked his way through
Franny's books and piles of clothes to his side of the
room and began taking off his pajamas. And I'm probably the only boy in the world who's neater than his
sister, he thought.

When he was younger, Martin had dreamed of

building a brick wall down the middle of their bedroom. When you share a room, you share everything — friends, toys, and diseases. Good thing diabetes
isn't catching, Martin thought. When Franny got the
measles, I got the measles. When she got the chicken
pox, I got the chicken pox. She's very generous with
her diseases, Martin thought.

Martin began to dress. Do I need gym shoes? he
wondered. No, he answered himself. Today is Friday — finally. Tuesday had seemed like Friday.
Wednesday had seemed like Friday and so had Thurs-
day. Now it was Friday and already he was tired of
Friday.

If it's Friday, Martin thought, it's report time. He
picked a balled-up sock from the floor, pulled it into
shape, and started to put it on. Whew! Martin thought.
This really stinks. And so do reports.

Mr. Raven, his teacher, was very big on reports.
Reports, reports, reports. All they ever did was reports. At the beginning of the year, they'd been fun.
But lately Martin could never decide what he wanted
to write about. And when he did think of something,
he couldn't write down what was in his head. When
he wrote down his ideas they sounded stupid.

Reports are stupid, Martin decided, zipping his
jeans. Every Monday Mr. Raven assigned a report due
on Friday. This week the topic was animals. Martin
had spent the whole week trying to decide what animal
he wanted to write about. Finally, last night, he thought
he would do a report on ravens. Ravens are mysterious
and dark, he'd reasoned. Besides, he wanted to see
how Mr. Raven would react.

But Martin's favorite show had been on TV and he didn't finish the report. All he had was the first line he'd copied from the dictionary: "Any of several heavy-billed, dark birds, larger than crows, of the genus *Corvus,* species *Corax,* family Corvidae." He didn't know what every word meant, but at least it didn't sound dumb.

Mr. Raven will probably get angry, he thought. I don't care. He slipped on his shirt with a shrug. Lately, he seems angry with me about everything. Martin tied his shoes with double knots and walked into the kitchen.

For the past couple of months Martin's life had been crowded with problems — loud, noisy problems that jostled one another rudely inside his head, that sounded like his parents arguing before his father left, yelling at the same time so he couldn't understand what either of them was saying.

Franny had the morning paper spread all over the kitchen table and was poring over the opinion page, completely absorbed in an editorial.

"Hey, Martin," Franny said, looking up. "Listen to this. It says here that no place in the world is free of pollution. Why, they've even found nicotine from tobacco smoke in snow down in Antarctica. That's really something!"

She read on, out loud, and Martin tuned her out. He fixed himself a bowl of cereal and plopped into a chair opposite Franny. We *never* have good cereal, he thought. He dumped three spoonfuls of sugar on his cereal. Then he dumped on a fourth. He poured milk on top and watched the sugar disappear. If we had good cereal, she'd eat it. He looked at Franny and took a bite of cereal.

". . . some pollution stays in the stratosphere indefinitely, trapping heat like a greenhouse . . ."

Martin closed his eyes and, holding his mouth still, felt sugar melt in his mouth and drip off the edges of his tongue.

If Franny would shut up, he thought, I'd eat my socks for breakfast. Without any sugar.

But since his father had left, Franny had started to discuss the editorials with *him*. Half the time he didn't want to hear about the world's problems — inflation, famine, pollution, nuclear weapons. He had his own problems. He didn't need anybody else's.

Martin didn't know all the reasons why his parents had separated. All he knew was that, for a long time, his parents hadn't acted like adults at all. They'd acted worse than when he and Franny were little and fought over the plastic shovel in their sandbox. He looked at Franny as she read and remembered one night when he and Franny were in bed and her face was frozen into a frown like the one on her face now. He'd been lying on his back, wide-eyed and shivering even though he was covered with blankets and the room was warm. They could hear the muffled sound of their parents fighting. They'd heard their mother scream at their father, "All you ever think about is yourself! You're nothing but a selfish, irresponsible bastard!"

A crash splintered the two heartbeats of silence that followed. And then they heard their father say, in a beer-soaked voice, "You've changed, Pat. You're as exciting as a dead fish." His father had left that night. He'd come back during the next couple of days only to pack his tools into a U-Haul. And then he'd left for good.

My family is now like the fraction story problems we're studying in school, Martin thought, taking a deep breath: If one fourth of a family now lives in Alaska and three fourths of that family still live at home, how many people in the family are happy?

My family is a story problem that doesn't make any sense, he thought. No more sense than my father leaving.

Martin looked up at the empty chair where his father had always sat. Suddenly Martin missed his dad so much his heart felt as if somebody were using it for a punching bag. Stop that, Martin scolded himself, taking a deep breath. I'm miserable and it's Dad's fault. Martin glared hatefully at the chair.

Martin pictured his father working in their garage, which was loaded with more power tools hanging from the walls and sitting on benches than the Sears store downtown. In his mind's eye, Martin saw his father leaning over a bench, planing a piece of wood. Golden ribbons curled from the plane, covering his dad's hands like a fleece.

Martin remembered how he and his best friend Barney practiced for hours with planes and scraps of wood. Barney could soon plane curls of wood so thin that light shone through them. Martin's dad had been very impressed. But Martin wasn't very good with his hands or with tools. His curls were always thin on one side and so thick on the other that the wood cracked sideways as it curled. No matter how many times his father showed him, Martin couldn't get it right.

Frustrated, his dad had finally held Martin's hands with his own sandpapery fingers. "These are girl hands," his father had said, disgusted. Remembering this, Martin's hands shook and milk slopped from his spoon onto his chin. He looked down at his hands. They were smooth and soft and pink — unlike his father's hands, which were always etched with grease-blackened wrinkles. Martin looked at his fingernails. They were clean and shiny, with a moon rising from the bottom of each one. His father's fingernails were always rimmed with dirt and at least one of them was always purple-black from a hammer or bump.

Martin scooped some cereal and milk into his spoon. He longed to be able to work with tools the way his father did. As Martin lifted the spoon to his mouth he pictured the curls of wood piling up light and fluffy and dripping like golden soap bubbles to the floor. Just as he stuck the spoon in his mouth, his father's face was suddenly replaced with Barney's face. Martin's throat tightened and he gasped, inhaling some of the milk. Martin held his breath, quickly swallowed, and then burst out coughing.

"Are you all right?" Franny said, looking up from the newspaper.

Martin nodded, tears streaming down his cheeks. He swallowed and breathed carefully, trying not to tickle his throat and cough. He wiped his cheeks with the back of his hand and looked down at his cereal bowl. Barney, he thought, his breathing more relaxed. He was always right in the thick of whatever Dad was doing — handing Dad the right-size crescent wrench or the snub-nosed pliers or catching the trim from the table saw.

Whenever I tried to help I drilled holes crooked, Martin thought. And most of the time I cut wood on the wrong side of the line. Barney and Dad went well together, Martin thought — like father and son. I tried to understand Dad's jokes, but mostly I laughed when Barney did. They were special together — Dad and Barney. I wanted to be special too, Martin thought. But I wasn't.

Martin lifted his bowl and tipped it toward his mouth. He let the thick, milky syrup run into his mouth. As he put down the bowl, Martin looked up at Franny. She was reading the front page of the newspaper, frowning and chasing the text down the columns with her finger. Martin got up, put his cereal bowl in the sink, and ran water into it. She doesn't have enough problems to worry about, Martin thought. So she reads about other people's problems in the paper.

I used to be able to talk to Barney and feel better about things, Martin thought, looking out the window over the sink. But that's impossible. He hates my guts. And I wouldn't have him for a friend if he was the last person on earth. Not since the Saturday after Dad left.

Martin thought about that Saturday. Barney had wanted to go skating on Onion Creek and Martin had just wanted to be alone. He'd tried to talk Barney out of it, saying that the ice wasn't thick enough. But when Barney called him a wimp, Martin couldn't back down. He had to go.

The air was so cold it tickled the back of Martin's throat when he breathed in. The grass looked freezer-burned and the trees shivered in the wind. He carried his hockey skates, the laces tied together, slung over his shoulder. He and Barney said very little as they walked into the woods.

They put on their skates, sitting on a muscled root that jutted out from the bank and then dropped down into the ice like a bent leg. Stashing their boots in the hollow underneath the root, they stepped out onto the ice.

"Looks solid to me," Barney said, stamping one skate. The ice popped and a dark hairline crack shot out from his skate toward the opposite bank.

Carefully at first, and then more boldly, they skated up the creek, teeth and bones chattering when they hit frozen riffles. Sometimes they had to step over logs and flotsam locked in the ice, hearing water gurgle underneath. For a while, Martin completely forgot about his parents. He and Barney chased each other around the smooth stretches of ice, yelling and whooping, their breath billowing like two steam engines, their fingers and toes tingling. Sometimes they hit patches of ice covered with a thin layer of dirt blown from the bank, which made them grind to sudden stops and caused them to fall.

"Look at this!" Barney called, throwing up an arch of shaved ice as he stopped near the bank. "The ice looks like lace!"

Martin skated up and peered down. It did. Tiny needles of ice crisscrossed in delicate embroidered patterns just below a skin of clear ice. Farther down, Martin saw dark water pulsing like blood. How beautiful, Martin thought, shifting his weight so that he could get a closer look.

Splintering like a smashed window, the ice dropped out from under Martin and he fell into the creek up to his knees.

"Yeow!" Martin yelled, the cold water biting his skin. He scrambled toward the bank and climbed out. His jeans stiffened and crinkled as the water froze. Shivering uncontrollably, Martin glared at Barney, who had pushed farther out, onto more solid ice. "I told you the ice wasn't thick enough!"

"It's not my fault!" Barney said, shrugging. "You should have been more careful."

Without thinking, Martin yelled, "All you ever think about is yourself! You're nothing but a selfish, inconsiderate bastard!" His voice, trembling from cold and anger, sounded just like his mother's.

They didn't say anything as they made their way back to their boots. Martin struggled to pull off his skates. Running home, Martin felt as if beanbags had been stuffed into his boots.

After that, their friendship went flat, like soda sitting in a glass.

At school they ignored each other until one day, after lunch, Martin walked by as Barney was showing off for Carrie, who had just moved from New Jersey. Barney was doing fake karate chops and moves, his face contorted, his jaw moving up and down and sideways like a grasshopper chewing, his arms waving like a grasshopper's antennae, his fingers held like a grasshopper's feet. Barney blocked Martin's path and crouched, his feet wide apart. "Hi-*ya!*" Barney cried, looking over at Carrie to make sure she was watching.

Without thinking, Martin kicked Barney in the balls. With an expression that melted from shock to pain, Barney doubled over. Martin stood, frozen, not believing what he'd done. He wanted to help but, before he could move, Carrie ran up to Barney. "Are you all right?" she asked breathlessly.

"I'm going to get you for that," Barney whispered to Martin through clenched teeth.

"It was an accident," Martin said in a numbed whisper.

"I'm going to get you. . . ."

And he had, several times. Just yesterday Barney pulled the oldest trick in the book — he put a tack on Martin's seat. When he sat on it, Martin had thought about Franny giving him a shot.

*   *   *

I deserved that, Martin thought, turning from the kitchen window. Now we're even.

Martin started walking toward the door when his mother swooped into the kitchen dressed in her "woman-executive-on-the-rise" suit. She was brushing her hair with one hand and patting it into place with her other hand. "Remember, Marty, I'll be late tonight from work and you should help Franny with dinner."

Again? Martin thought.

The week after his father moved out, Martin's

mother started taking evening classes at the university. She wanted to complete her degree in horticulture so that she could quit her executive secretary job and, maybe, open a nursery.

She *never* has time to cook anymore, Martin thought glumly. Not even bothering to say good morning or good-bye, Martin put on his jacket and stepped out into the spring day, slamming the kitchen door behind him.

The sky was powder blue, the air was cool and moist, and the daffodils were blooming. The buds on the trees were swelling, ready to burst into leaves. Birds were singing.

Spring makes me sick, he thought. While spring is being so beautiful, making things green and covering up winter trash, I'm stuck in school listening to some dumb teacher and doing dumb assignments and fighting with dumb people who used to be my friends.

Spring, spring, spring, spring. Cute, cute, cute, cute.

He closed his eyes and thought about how his day had begun. *Click.* The sound ricocheted in his head and he wished the days would click on and off, day and night and day and night, until he was grown up.

# Chapter 2

"Yikes!" Tom Raven jumped as the alarm clock went off. His heart galloped like a runaway horse as he grabbed for the clock. But he couldn't move.

"What the . . . " Mr. Raven's eyes flashed open and he kicked his legs but the blankets were wound tightly around his body. He panicked, thrashing like a fish in the bottom of a boat, wrestling to untangle himself from the ropy embrace of his blanket and sheet. The blanket's grip on his legs reluctantly loosened but the stranglehold of the sheet around his neck tightened. Tom Raven twisted, reared, and flopped. With a tremendous grunt, he flung off the sheet. He sat in the middle of his bed, gasping, the angry buzz of his electric alarm clock drilling into his head.

"Oh, shut up!" Raven exploded. He swatted at the alarm clock, missed, and swatted again. It flew across his tiny bedroom. The cord rippled through the air and lay like a dead snake on the floor. Silence filled the room so quickly that Raven thought perhaps he'd suddenly gone deaf. He breathed in and heard his nose whistling. Whew! he thought, breathing out.

What a night! Mr. Raven had struggled half the night to get to sleep and when he finally did, he had weird dreams.

In one dream his head had been a bowling ball, bouncing down a polished wooden lane. The world spun around in a colorful blur and then jumped every time his nose or chin hit the lane. Feeling dizzy in the dream, Mr. Raven closed his eyes and the dizziness went away. Still dreaming, he opened his eyes just in time to see the pins loom ahead. Each pin was a student in his class and . . . CRASH! they flew in every direction.

Before he knew it, his head was rumbling along in the dark on a conveyor belt. The belt spit him out into glaring light and he found himself looking up at a shadowy face that was creased with a twisted smile. Hands reached down and picked up Mr. Raven's head, brushing the hair from his sweaty forehead. Mr. Raven gagged as a dirty-tasting thumb hooked into his mouth, pressing up into the pallet. And he winced as clawlike fingers reached for his eyes.

Just then, the alarm clock had gone off. Raven shuddered and shook his head. He'd been having a lot of weird dreams lately, but that was definitely the weirdest. Having dreams like that sapped Mr. Raven's confidence. It was Friday and he didn't feel up to standing in front of a roomful of kids. It made him feel like the conductor of a band whose members were facing every which way and trying to blow through the wrong ends of their instruments.

As Mr. Raven sat on the edge of his bed and stood up, he wished he was sick or kidnapped or anything but having to go to school. If I'd known what some days of teaching were going to be like, he thought, I'd have majored in basket weaving instead of teaching — speaking Chinese with a French accent, the history of toilet paper, spinning and knitting clothes-dryer lint . . . *anything* but teaching.

I used to like teaching, he thought. He stumbled into the bathroom and reached into the shower stall. He turned on the water, tested it, and stepped into its warm, soothing spray. He felt a soggy heaviness tugging at his waist and looked down as his water-logged pajama bottoms fell with a heavy "ker-plop" around his feet. He stepped out of them and kicked them to the side of the shower stall. He wrestled out of the clinging tops and threw them on top of the bottoms.

Mr. Raven tilted his face directly into the shower and slowly breathed out of his nose and mouth. Whatever possessed me to teach anyway? he wondered, letting the water rush over his face. Teaching kids swimming over the summer was one thing, he thought. I liked being with kids and laughing with them. I loved to watch them gain confidence in themselves. And, I have to admit, I liked the way kids looked up to me. Lifting his face from the spray, Mr. Raven breathed in.

But I should have known teaching fifth grade would be a mistake. My fifth grade was miserable. That was the year, Mr. Raven remembered, bowing his head to soak his hair and enjoying the feel of water running off his back, that some smart aleck started calling me the Ravin' Maniac and Bird Brain. A little fifth-grade humor, Mr. Raven thought grimly. Fifth-grade humor that had lasted through fifth grade and sixth grade. Most people's humor never grows up beyond fifth grade, he thought. If that kid hadn't moved to another town the summer before seventh grade, people might still be calling me the Ravin' Maniac and thinking it was clever.

He poured shampoo into the palm of his hand and massaged it into his scalp. *This is one way to take the kinks out of one's brain.* He sighed. His whole body relaxed.

He smiled. In all fairness to the kid who started calling him the Ravin' Maniac and Bird Brain, Mr. Raven thought, I *was* a strange fifth grader. Most of the kids in his school chased one another around the playground. What Mr. Raven had liked to do, though, was run around by himself with his arms held out like wings. It had nothing to do with his name being Raven. He just liked the way the air felt sweeping over and under his arms. He could pretend he was swooping through the clouds and he liked the way his unzipped jacket rode up on his shoulders, billowed sideways, and flapped behind him like a cape.

He rinsed off the shampoo and grabbed the soap. I could do this all day, Mr. Raven thought — take inventory of my body. He stooped to wash his toes. The water beat on his back. The sweet perfume of the soap caused Mr. Raven to imagine himself in a warm rain, bending over to smell flowers. All present and accounted for, he thought, counting each toe as he washed between them.

Mr. Raven watched the soapy water curl into the drain, the bubbles following one another single file. I wish I could wash this past year down the drain, he thought, moving up to his ankles and then his knees. Looking back on it, this year in Clifton has been harder than any of my previous four. Sometimes I feel more inexperienced than a student teacher and less respected than a substitute teacher.

I just haven't been myself lately, he thought, carefully washing between his legs. Ever since the divorce, he felt jumbled up inside, as if somebody — perhaps his ex-wife, Phoebe — had reached inside him and rearranged his organs. He sometimes felt as if his stomach had surrounded his heart like an amoeba and was slowly digesting it. Sometimes he felt that his intestines had wiggled and squirmed their way into the place where his lungs should be. He lathered his chest and the bubbles turned his chest hair white. After he and Phoebe separated, he found himself craving new faces, as he craved fresh air while visiting a big city. So he'd moved . . . to Clifton. Mr. Raven had moved with the same sense of adventure he felt when he went on vacations. But, like a vacation, after a couple of weeks he found himself longing for the familiar faces and streets of his hometown. He missed the house he'd left behind — the faint smells of coffee, spices, and baking bread in the kitchen, the chirplike creak when he stepped on the front porch step third from the top, the view from the upstairs bedroom, which didn't end with the town but kept going over the rolling cornfields that changed from black to green to yellow to white with the seasons.

Mr. Raven strained to reach the middle of his back. All the changes in his life had taken their toll. The divorce had been a huge change. And then came the move and trying to make friends in this small town where everybody seemed to have grown up with friends and didn't have time for new ones. And then came trying to teach completely new kids and working with parents he didn't know and who didn't know him. All of these things had whittled away at his teaching. Frankly, he scolded himself while he scrubbed his armpits, I'm not being as good a teacher as I can be.

For one thing, Mr. Raven decided, he could barely muster the energy to keep ahead of the kids. Kids are kids, he thought. They aren't always sweet or honest or eager to learn or quick to obey or enthusiastic. They scribble on each other's art projects, spit into each other's milk at lunch, swear like their parents, are unhappy when they are forced to work and bored when they aren't forced to do something.

Usually I can handle all that, Mr. Raven thought, scrubbing his face. But this year, I'm tired of the constant battle between kids and teacher. I'm tired of always having to win.

Even his new principal, Mr. Clove, had been

quick to pick up on all of this. After a couple of days, Mr. Clove hinted that perhaps the "noise and activity" level in Mr. Raven's class was a little too high. Of course, Mr. Raven thought, Mr. Clove would be happiest if the kids acted in class the same way they'd act at a funeral. But kids are kids, he thought again. And nothing will change that.

So kids aren't perfect, Mr. Raven thought, rinsing the soap out of his ears. So teachers aren't perfect. So life isn't perfect. So?

Maybe all of that will change, he sighed, stepping out of the shower and grabbing a towel. Last week, on Friday, he'd finally received the divorce papers from Phoebe by registered mail. He'd signed them, his hand shaking from relief, anger, pain, and sorrow.

Mr. Raven shook his head sadly as he folded the damp towel and hung it on the rack. It's over. Now, maybe I can throw myself into teaching.

And what about the rest of the day? he asked himself. It is Friday . . . at last. The reports I assigned on Monday are due this afternoon. Probably half of them won't be done. And one student hadn't turned in an honest-to-goodness report for the past four or five weeks.

Mr. Raven wiped steam off the mirror above the sink with his towel. He admired his foggy reflection. What would be Martin's excuse today? Mr. Raven pinched up his face and bobbed his head back and forth. *Our set of encyclopedias is missing the T's and I couldn't do my autobiographical report on turkeys. I took notes at the library but when I got home I couldn't read my handwriting. I forgot. I thought you*

*said next Friday. I put it on our home computer and
the computer ate the floppy disk.*

I'll floppy-disk him, Mr. Raven thought as he got
his razor and shaving cream from the medicine cabinet. I bet his family doesn't even have a computer.

Mr. Raven leaned toward the mirror as he spread
a beard of shaving cream on his face. As he stared into
the mirror, the image from last night's nightmare flashed
in his head. That face, he thought. That face and that
smile . . . that face was Martin's! He picked up his
razor and, scrunching his mouth toward his left ear,
he started swiping at his right cheek.

Careful, he told himself. Slow down. Don't shave
off everything else along with the beard. But even
while he tried to calm himself, Mr. Raven felt the
sting of anger as he scraped too hard against the tender
skin along the underside of his jaw. Martin made him
angry, simple as that. In five years of teaching, Martin
was the first really good student Mr. Raven had met
who'd suddenly soured and stopped working.

At first, for a week or two, Mr. Raven just ignored
Martin's lack of interest in school. And then he'd invited Martin into the classroom for a "business lunch."
Usually, business lunches were fun. The one with Martin was a flop. The boy didn't respond to any of Mr.
Raven's questions or jokes, didn't talk about whatever
was bothering him. Didn't smile even once.

Even though Martin continued to withdraw in
class, Mr. Raven kept hoping that his problem would
pass. But when his mood got even worse, Mr. Raven
stopped worrying and became irritated.

A few times, Mr. Raven wanted to physically shake

Martin, tell him to stop playing this stupid game. It made Martin look bad . . . and it made Mr. Raven look bad. At such times, Mr. Raven would flash back to his own fifth-grade teacher, a woman with a wrinkled voice but a smooth, grim face. She would tweak his ear and say, "Is this how you turn your brain on in the morning, Tom? Looks like you forgot again today." And she would give his ear another half twist and smile when he grimaced.

Mr. Raven took a final swipe with the razor. It's dangerous to think of Martin and shave at the same time, he thought. Look, I'm already frustrated and angry and shaky and school hasn't even started yet. I could have cut off my chin.

Mr. Raven leaned closer to the mirror. Look at that. My face used to be as smooth as a new eraser. Now I've got furrows on my forehead you could plant corn in — from worrying about kids. Mr. Raven squinted. And the bags under my eyes are beginning to look like baby burlap sacks. I got those from having weird dreams and tossing and turning all night.

Yes, he thought, testing a grin in the mirror. Teaching is definitely hazardous to your health. Mr. Raven frowned. It probably causes cancer. But somebody's got to do it.

He looked closer in the mirror as he patted the excess foam off his face. *Is that a pimple?* Raven sighed. I'm too old for pimples. Maybe that comes from being around fifth graders so much. Sometimes I feel like I never graduated from fifth grade. Each year my body thinks it's starting puberty again. Maybe puberty is contagious, Raven thought.

Without thinking, just as he used to do when he was in junior high, he squeezed the pimple and popped it. I hope I'm not going to regret this, he thought, wiping pimple juice off the mirror. I hope this isn't going to fester.

Raven looked at his watch. He was late. He quickly dressed in clothes he'd dropped on his bedroom floor because they weren't quite dirty enough to go into the clothes hamper, which was buried under a pile of clothes anyway. He didn't have time to make a sandwich or eat breakfast. Maybe somebody will bring cookies or treats for the teacher's lounge, he hoped.

I'm lucky I live so close to school, he thought. If I run I'll make it. He rushed out the door, carrying corrected papers in both hands and a banana sticking straight out of his mouth.

Damn! I forgot to put on deodorant, he thought. But he kept running.

# Chapter 3

Martin felt as if he was trapped in a stalled car in the blazing sun with the windows rolled up. The room was hot and stuffy and his desk was too small. He shifted his weight and fidgeted. He straightened his legs, but couldn't stretch or relax. He listened to Mr. Raven's chalk clicking on the blackboard.

Martin gazed at the deep blue sky and the puffy clouds that moved slowly from one window to the next without changing shape. When he turned his eyes inside, the classroom was like a cave, and Mr. Raven reminded him of a wild caveman drawing dinosaurs on a shadowy cave wall. Martin's eyes slowly adjusted to the dark and he saw Mr. Raven scribbling next week's vocabulary words on the blackboard for the class to copy. Too bad Mr. Raven isn't drawing a dinosaur, Martin thought. He'd make a great caveman.

Martin wrote down the vocabulary words — *adolescence, futile, infamous, minuscule, aggravate.* "Aggravate." Martin sounded the word in his head as he wrote it down. That's what Barney does to me, he thought. Like this morning, first thing. Martin remembered walking into the schoolyard, where Barney and two other boys from his class, Clyde and Harold, cornered him against the playground's chain-link fence. Before Martin could escape, Clyde and Harold grabbed Martin's arms, right below his armpits. Martin tried to wriggle away but they dug their thumbs into the tender undersides of his upper arms, pinching a nerve against the bone. Then they pushed Martin against the fence and Barney reached down the back of Martin's jeans, grabbed the elastic top of his underwear, and yanked up, as if he were starting a lawn mower. Barney nearly pulled Martin off the ground as the underwear grabbed him tight. Martin struggled and his underwear grabbed more tightly. He groaned.

When Clyde and Harold let go, Martin lost his balance and tumbled forward, right into a puddle of water.

"What'd you do that for?" Martin said, looking up and grimacing. "We were even."

"Just thought you'd like to know." Barney's smile was as sinister as his voice. "That's called the 'Nutcracker Suite.' " Barney turned and walked away toward Carrie, who was giggling by the school building.

I'll show him, Martin remembered thinking as he picked himself up and wiped his hands on the front of his jeans. He had taken a step to steady himself and felt a crunching under his foot. Martin stepped back and looked at the asphalt. He saw a dried worm that had baked on the playground. He stooped and picked it up. It grew vaguely slimy in his damp fingers. He stuck the worm in his jacket pocket and reached for another.

Martin quickly copied the rest of the words on his paper.

"We will have a pretest on Monday," he heard Mr. Raven say. "The final will be a week from today." And then Mr. Raven said the words he'd been waiting for: "Please get out your reading books." Martin raised his hand. "Yes?" Mr. Raven asked.

"I think my book's out in my locker," Martin said. "Can I go look?"

"I don't know. *Can* you?" Martin heard Carrie snicker. He hated that word game teachers always played with students.

"*May* I go look in my locker?"

"Yes," Mr. Raven said.

As Martin walked toward his locker, his heart began to pound. His locker was right next to Barney's.

Most kids ate the school's hot lunches. But Barney's parents, especially his father, who was a doctor, were persnickety about what Barney ate. They didn't allow him to eat the school's hot lunches. So Barney brought his lunch instead. Every day he brought the same things: some kind of soup in a thermos, a homemade-bread sandwich wrapped in waxed paper because the bread was too big to fit into a regular sandwich bag, and some fruit or a granola bar.

Looking up and down the hall to make sure nobody was watching, Martin opened his locker and took out his jacket. Quietly, he opened Barney's locker and took out the lunch box. Kneeling on the floor, Martin opened the box, took out the thermos, and unscrewed the lid. A plume of steam curled up. Martin smelled chicken noodle. Perfect, he thought. He reached into his jacket pocket. The dried worms he'd picked up on the playground were paralyzed in painful-looking kinks. One by one he dropped them into the thermos. He counted nine satisfying plops.

Martin screwed on the lid, stuffed the thermos back in the lunch box, and put the box back into Barney's locker. He closed the locker door, lifting the latch so that it didn't clang.

Martin quickly checked his own locker to see if his reading book was there. As he suspected, it wasn't. Martin threw his jacket on top of all the graded assignments he hadn't taken home, closed the door, and walked back to the classroom. He tried not to smile.

"No luck?" Mr. Raven asked, not even looking up from his papers as Martin walked into the room.

"No." Martin wrestled the upturned corners of his mouth into a frown.

"That's too bad." Mr. Raven looked at Martin and stood up. "I'd like you to look on with Barney while we discuss the story." Mr. Raven's eyes swept over the class. "Time for reading. Please turn to page two hundred and four. . . ."

*Is Mr. Raven doing this on purpose?* Martin dragged a chair over to Barney's desk. He looked into Barney's face — a face that Martin knew better than his own. He thought about the worms and felt a pang of guilt. Barney muttered something that Martin couldn't understand and opened the reading book.

What had gone wrong? Martin wondered. Was it

his fault or Barney's fault that they didn't get along anymore? Or was it his dad's fault?

Barney turned the reading book so that Martin had to twist his head to see. Half listening, unable to read, Martin thought about the time he and Barney searched for golf balls in Skunk River, which curled lazily through Clifton's golf course.

That day they'd hiked through the golf-course woods and were standing on a hill above the river, watching golfers hit balls down the fairway that crossed the water. Sometimes the balls arched over the river and landed on the other side. But balls often skidded on the water's surface and were swallowed up into its muddy folds.

They decided they could retrieve some of those balls and sell them to golfers who lost their balls in the river. They climbed down to the riverbank, took off their shoes and socks, and eased their legs into the lukewarm water.

"We'll find them with our feet," Barney said.

Wiggling his toes, feeling the mud ooze and squish, Martin tried to distinguish between rounded rocks and golf balls. It was hard but, reaching his arm down up to his armpit, he retrieved three balls and only one rock.

"How many have you got?" he called back to Barney, who was behind him and closer to the opposite bank.

"I've got three crawdaddies and two electric eels," Barney called back. "How many have you got?"

"A billion and one," Martin called.

Barney grinned and began prancing in the water, lifting his knees high, almost clearing the water with his feet. "Help! I'm being attacked by killer kissing fish! Help! Stop kissing. Help! Help! They're kissing me to death!"

"Keep them busy while I escape." Martin laughed. He turned around and tried to run away, but the water pushed against the front of his thighs and calves like giant, underwater hands. He could hear Barney splashing and yelling about the kissing fish being worse than girls.

"Yeow!"

Martin stopped and leaned into the current. Trying to keep his balance, he turned and saw Barney hobble toward the bank.

"I think I stepped on something!" Barney scrambled up. The bottom of his foot was bright red, with blood dripping off his toes into the water.

Barney had stepped on the jagged edge of a broken bottle, Martin remembered, twisting his head so that he could see where the class was in the story. He had helped stop the bleeding by tightly wrapping Barney's foot in his T-shirt. A golfer drove them to the clubhouse, where they called Barney's mother. The gash took eight stitches. Martin went back later that day and picked up the shoes.

He looked up at Barney's face. We could be friends, you know, he said silently.

\* \* \*

Lunchtime finally came. The class walked down the hall, single file, just as Mr. Raven liked. Clyde walked behind Martin, trying to step on the heels of Martin's shoes. Martin quickened his step so Clyde wouldn't give him a flat tire.

The lunchroom smells grew stronger, reminding Martin of the neighbor's garbage after their baby arrived several months ago — a combination of sour milk, bacon grease, and dirty diapers.

During the rest of the school day, the lunchroom was used as a gymnasium. The tables were folded into the walls and the basketball hoops were lowered. The windows were opened to let in fresh air. But, even so, the gymnasium always smelled like the inside of a refrigerator that had rotten lettuce slime in the crisper.

"Hey, watch where you're going," Clyde said, bumping his tray against Martin's in the line.

"Yeah." Carrie was in line behind Clyde. "Watch it."

Martin turned around to glare at Clyde. Clyde's hair looked as if moths had eaten away at it. "Not much to watch," Martin said, turning around.

Barney was always the first one at the table reserved for Mr. Raven's class. Every day he sat on the outside edge of the table so he would be the first out the door for noon recess. When Martin and Barney were friends, Barney had always saved the spot next to him for Martin. Lately Barney had been saving that spot for Carrie.

Martin sat as far from Barney as he could — next to the wall. He sat at an angle so that he could glance at Barney every couple of seconds out of the corner of his eye.

This has got to taste worse than worms, Martin thought, chewing the chili con carne carefully, as though it might have glass in it. Martin watched Barney take out his thermos and unscrew the cup top and the lid. Martin's heart quickened. He swallowed. Maybe I shouldn't have done that, he thought.

He watched Barney pour soup into the cup top. The chili went down Martin's throat in a big lump, like a ball of grease and hair and scum slowly passing through a drain pipe.

I could stop him, Martin thought. He watched in fascination and horror as Barney lifted a spoonful of soup to his mouth. A dark, limp strand hung over the edge of Barney's spoon. The spoon disappeared into Barney's mouth and reappeared empty.

Barney chewed thoughtfully, listening to Carrie. Suddenly Barney's eyes started and his jaw dropped as if he were trying to keep something in his mouth from touching his tongue. He gagged, dropped his spoon, and spit his soup into his cupped hands. He looked at the half-chewed mass in his hands and gagged again. Soup leaked through his fingers and dripped onto the table.

Carrie stopped talking and peered into Barney's hands. "That looks like . . . worms," she said. She moved away from Barney and bumped into Clyde.

Barney continued staring at his hands, and his face turned bright red. "Worms!" he bellowed. And then he looked at Martin.

Martin pursed his quivering lips so tightly that they disappeared. Barney looked down at his hands again and then back at Martin. His face drained to white. The lunchroom was strangely quiet. A few kids poked at their chile con carne, looking for worms.

"Is anything wrong?" The lunchroom monitor, Ms. Pendle, who was also the school librarian, strode up to Barney. She leaned forward to look into Barney's hands and quickly straightened, a stricken look on her face. "My word. What is *that?*"

Barney's eyes watered. A piece of noodle was stuck on his chin. He kept staring at Martin. "Worms," he muttered. "Somebody put worms in my soup."

Ms. Pendle's face followed Barney's gaze toward Martin. Martin quickly looked down and shoveled chili into his mouth. Now I've done it, Martin thought. He felt the chili wriggling around in his stomach. Why did I do that? Martin scolded himself. Barney was my friend.

Martin's stomach writhed and a big burp bubbled up. Ugh! Martin thought. He swallowed hard, trying to force it down, and suddenly he began to hiccup.

Martin looked up. Barney was crawling out from the table's bench, holding his hands in front of him. Ms. Pendle was still looking at Martin, squinting her eyes, thinking.

"Martin," she said. Barney stood next to her. "Do you know anything about this?" She pointed toward Barney's cupped hands with her chin, which was as sharp as her voice.

"Hic!" Martin breathed deeply. "No." He hiccupped again.

"Well," Ms. Pendle said, "I'd like you to help Barney get cleaned up."

"No!" Barney said. He looked as though he was going to cry. "I'll take care of myself." Ms. Pendle frowned but didn't say anything. She turned and marched Barney toward the hall.

"Hic!" Martin looked at the cold chili hardening in his tray. "Hic!" He smiled. The hiccups tore at his insides. He opened his carton of milk, held his breath, closed his eyes, and took a couple of swallows. Yuck! he thought. I hate warm milk.

Martin put down his carton and held his breath until he thought he would burst. Opening his eyes, Martin slowly breathed out and slowly breathed in. His hiccups were gone.

He looked around the room. Everything seemed back to normal. Carrie was talking to Clyde, who looked pleased that she was paying attention to him. Barney's open lunch box was on her other side. Steam still curled from the open top of the thermos. Thinking about the worms inside the thermos, Martin couldn't face another mouthful of lunch. He set the half-full carton of milk in front of him and spooned chili into it. He put down the spoon, reached for the Texas toast, ripped off a hunk, and began stuffing it into the carton's spout. Milk squished up and oozed over the spout's edge.

"And *what* do you think you're doing?" Martin jumped at the sound of Ms. Pendle's voice. *Why do teachers sneak up on kids?* It's not fair, Martin thought.

He cleared his throat. "I'm, uh, I'm cleaning up my tray."

"Yes, and for wasting perfectly good food you will help Mr. Thorne clean up the lunchroom." She walked over to Barney's things, packed them into his lunch box, and left.

As Martin mopped spilled milk under the first-graders' table, he was thankful for one thing: he didn't have to find out how Barney was going to get even with him on the playground.

When Martin finished in the lunchroom, Mr. Thorne sent him to his classroom. Mr. Raven looked up from the papers he was correcting as Martin walked in. He grunted, nodded his head, and went back to grading papers. Martin sat at his desk and laid his head on his desktop. Sometimes I don't even feel like I know myself anymore, he thought.

The bell rang. Kids poured into the room, bringing with them snatches of spring air. Martin lifted his head and looked over at Barney's seat. It was empty. He must have gone home sick, Martin thought. He looked at Carrie, who was glaring at him.

\* \* \*

The sun shone into the classroom, growing more intense as the afternoon wore on. Martin was supposed to be reading a chapter in his social studies book, but he began to feel as if he'd been sitting on a beach without a hat for hours. His head felt as expanded and taut as a beach ball left out in the sun.

The whole class was restless. Feet shuffled. Textbook pages turned faster and louder. Sighs punctuated the ticking of the clock, sounding like steam escaping from a radiator in winter. Desks creaked and the air grew hotter and stuffier. Martin felt as if he were breathing under a blanket. He wished that time would speed up so that the afternoon would be over. He also wished that time would slow down, so that Mr. Raven would never call on the class to give their reports. Actually he wanted time to sprint toward report time, leap over that last part of the day, and land directly in the middle of dinner, which Franny would have cooked all by herself.

As Martin pretended to read, turning a page every forty-five seconds on the dot, he tried to think of a good excuse for not having his report done. Why didn't I just do the report? he thought. Sometimes thinking of a good excuse is much harder.

Maybe I can blame it on Franny, he thought. *Franny went into insulin shock and we had to take her to the hospital.* No, he thought. Mr. Raven could check with Franny's teacher and find out that she's perfectly OK.

Maybe I should tell him that my mom was so proud of it that she took my report to work to show her boss. Hell, Martin thought, shaking his head. I just should have done my report.

Mr. Raven stood behind his desk and cleared his throat. "OK, class. Put away your books. If you haven't finished reading today's lesson, it's homework for the weekend. Quiz on Monday."

The class woke up slowly, like a stretching cat. Martin looked around the classroom. Some kids, like Carrie, had their reports neatly centered on top of their desks. Others, like Harold, didn't have anything on their desks. Like Martin, Harold was looking around the room to see who else hadn't done their reports.

"It's time to hand in your reports." Raven opened his grade book. "When I call your name, bring it up and tell the class a little about the animal you chose."

Martin held his breath and looked out of the classroom windows.

"The first one today will be . . . Martin."

Martin's breath sounded like a punctured balloon as he released it. *Why is he picking on me?*

"Mr. Raven," Martin said, looking at his desktop. "I don't have my report with me today."

Mr. Raven's heart pounded as if he'd just finished gulping three cups of coffee. "Why is that?" He tried to keep his voice from betraying his frustration.

"Well, I . . . I . . . when you said Friday, I thought you meant *next* Friday." Martin smiled weakly at Mr. Raven.

Mr. Raven counted to five. "And what is your report on?" he asked. He felt his voice growing taut, as if his anger were straining on a leash.

"Um, I'm doing it on . . ." Martin swallowed. *Should I or shouldn't I?* There's nothing wrong with my animal, he decided. He took a deep breath. "I'm doing it on ravens," he said quietly, meeting Mr. Raven's eyes with his own.

Mr. Raven stared. Ravens? Was Martin making a fifth-grade joke out of his name? Mr. Raven grew angry. Martin could be the best student in the class if he wanted, Mr. Raven thought as he stared. He saw emotions — fear, anger, insolence — shift on Martin's face, like slides shown too fast. *Why is he doing these things? It's not like him!*

"Ravens?" Mr. Raven asked. Say no, he pleaded silently. But Martin nodded.

"Is that your idea of a joke?" Mr. Raven tried to smile but his voice strained to yell. "What kind of information were you looking for? My mother's first name? If I came from a brown egg or a white egg or a *speckled* egg? If I was a *crow* until I got big enough to be a *raven*?" Some of the kids in the class snickered. Mr. Raven blushed, remembering the boy who had called him Bird Brain. He paced up and down the length of the blackboard.

"Martin," he said, "I do not appreciate this kind of joke."

Martin watched Mr. Raven. He opened his mouth to tell Mr. Raven that he thought ravens were interesting animals and nothing came out but a raspy squawk.

"I'd like you to meet me after school," Mr. Raven said. "We have some things to discuss." He stopped pacing and took a deep breath. "Frank, I guess you're first," he said, hollowly.

Oh, boy, Martin thought, looking at his white knuckles. I've done it now.

\* \* \*

Without kids, the classroom seemed darker and larger. Martin watched Mr. Raven erase everything on the board except the names of the kids who hadn't done their reports. His name was at the top.

Mr. Raven clapped his hands to get rid of chalk dust as he turned around. "Martin," he said, walking toward Martin's desk. He squeezed into the seat of the desk in front of Martin and turned sideways, his legs in the aisle. "Martin, I think it's time I talked to your mother about how you've been doing lately." Mr. Raven looked at his hands. "This makes the fifth report in a row you haven't handed in. And you haven't done your reading for two weeks and you've flunked every math quiz since we started fractions a month ago." He looked up at Martin. "That's just not like you. I'm really puzzled . . . and frustrated . . . about what's happening." Mr. Raven examined Martin's face.

Martin looked down at his desktop. Mr. Raven's deodorant must have given up, Martin thought. Either that or it's called "Essence of Caveman." He tried not to smile. This was definitely not a good time to smile.

"Is something troubling you?"

Martin shook his head.

"You're sure?"

Martin didn't move.

"OK," Mr. Raven sighed. "You can go now."

Franny was waiting outside the school. There wasn't another kid in sight. "Heard you got yelled at today," she said, walking along beside him. "Boy, was that a dumb thing to do. I can't believe you did that." She sounded impressed. "You told him you were doing a report on . . ."

"Franny," Martin interrupted, "leave me alone. I already have a mother." And he ran down the sidewalk toward home.

# Chapter 4

Gray, rainy weather always makes the classroom glow, Mr. Raven thought. He stood by his desk in the back of the classroom and looked around. The faded construction paper on the bulletin boards released the bleach of trapped sunlight. The white letters on the green chalkboard vibrated and a fluorescent light fluttered on and off faster than Mr. Raven could blink his eyes.

Mr. Raven breathed deeply. The damp air sharpens classroom smells, he thought. He could almost taste the chalkiness of the air. He could smell somebody's wet hair, like a dog after swimming, only with a hint of shampoo. And somebody in the class needed to take a bath or wash their clothes.

The window next to Mr. Raven's desk was open. Breaths of air puffed in from outside as if a giant cat were sniffing at the window. Mr. Raven crossed his arms, hugged himself, and looked over the class. He enjoyed having his desk in the back of the classroom and being in control. He could watch the kids and they couldn't watch him.

A misty gust hit Mr. Raven's face like a sloppy kiss and papers on his desk skittered. He reached over and closed the window.

When he was in fifth grade, on days when the rain beat hypnotically on the roof, his head was strewn with thoughts as sodden as the rain-soaked leaves now plastered on the playground or smashed against its chain-link fence.

Mr. Raven turned his head and looked out the window. The trees, looking as stiff in their new leaves as a kid in new, unwashed jeans, shook their branches at the hovering clouds. The rain fell in blobs.

Mr. Raven felt somebody stare at him. He turned and saw Carrie standing in front of him, looking quizzically into his face.

"Ah . . . hello," Mr. Raven muttered, standing up. "May I help you, Carrie?"

She leaned toward him. "May I go to the bathroom?" she whispered.

Mr. Raven saw a pink wad at the side of her tongue. "Certainly," he said, smiling. "After you throw away your gum."

Carrie grimaced and nodded. That makes four times to the bathroom for Carrie today, he thought. Mr. Raven watched her turn, take the gum out of her mouth, and toss it into his wastebasket. But I can't say no. She's old enough to be having periods.

Mr. Raven scanned the room, getting his bearings. His eyes settled on Martin. Mr. Raven had been watching Martin all day, thinking about the conference he would hold after school with Martin's mother.

Mr. Raven thought back on the only time he'd met Martin's mother, during fall conferences. She'd just been to the dentist, where she'd had three cavities filled. Her tongue didn't quite work and her speech had been slightly slurred. A tiny dribble of saliva had leaked from a corner of her mouth during the conference and, because her lower lip was numb from Novocain, she couldn't feel the dripping. Mr. Raven remembered the dark patch on her purple blouse and how it grew into the shape of Africa. They had talked about what a wonderful student Martin was, he remembered — about how great Mr. Raven felt to have Martin in his class. Mr. Raven shook his head. *How was I supposed to know Martin would change so completely and so fast?*

He looked out the window. The rain had changed to a weepy drizzle. What went wrong? How could he tell Martin's mother that her son was now his biggest worry? How could he admit that he'd done everything he could think of and that nothing had worked? That he'd even had a helpless dream in which Martin used his head as a bowling ball? What if she tells me, like some parents, that he's fine at home and that if he's having problems at school that they're *my* problems?

Some of the kids were restless. Mr. Raven cleared his throat. "If you are finished, please use this time for independent reading." A few kids pulled books out of their desks.

He looked at Clyde. "And no comic books." Clyde

frowned, but he put the comic book back in his desk and took out a dog-eared paperback — the same one he'd been using all year. He turned to the first page.

Mr. Raven looked at the clock. Thank goodness the day is almost over, he thought.

Martin's attitude *had* improved today, he thought. During math Martin had brought a soggy, smeared handful of papers to Mr. Raven's desk.

"What is *this?*" Mr. Raven had asked, taking the spongy papers from Martin.

"My report," Martin said, "on . . . on ravens."

Mr. Raven carefully peeled the first page off the second page. "What happened?" Mr. Raven asked, looking up.

"Nothing," Martin mumbled, studying his feet.

"Nothing?"

"Well" — Martin softly sighed — "somebody threw it in a puddle."

"Who?"

Martin didn't say anything. He continued to study his feet.

"I see," Mr. Raven said. "Well, let's let these dry out and I'll look at it this afternoon."

When Mr. Raven announced that the class's pet rat, Mickey, needed to have his cage cleaned, Martin volunteered. It was the first time in a couple of months that Martin had volunteered for anything.

Mr. Raven smiled. Mickey loved to snuggle into pockets. Martin had put Mickey in his shirt pocket before he started cleaning the cage and, when he bent over to dump the yellow-stained newspaper into the garbage can, Mickey jumped onto the floor, scurried to a nearby corner bookshelf, and disappeared around the back.

"We'll find him," Mr. Raven had told Martin. "Mickey probably just needs a vacation." Like me, Mr. Raven had said to himself.

For the first time in a month or two, Martin had tried to answer some questions in class. Mr. Raven was so pleased, he called on Martin almost every time Martin's hand shot up. He was surprised at how much Martin had picked up the past month while appearing to be in a coma.

Mr. Raven looked up at the clock again. The last bell of the day was about to ring.

"OK, class," he said. "Let's straighten up the room so we can all go home." He watched the kids stuff books and papers in their desks. The room quieted as the class watched the clock's second hand creep slowly upward. . . .

BRRRIIING! Heads snapped to look at Mr. Raven. He counted to five, slowly, and whispered, "OK. . . ."

Kids jumped up from their desks and rushed for the door and Martin disappeared into the hall.

"Martin!" Mr. Raven called. Martin reappeared at the door. His raised eyebrows asked "Why?"

"I'd like you to copy your report on ravens while your mother and I talk." Mr. Raven walked to his desk and picked up the stack of papers. The papers looked like layers of puff pastry.

Martin trudged across the room, took the papers, turned, and bumped into his mother.

"Hello, Martin!" she panted.

"Hi," Martin said, hiding the papers behind his back. He looked at his feet.

"Hope I'm not late," Mrs. Enders said, looking at Mr. Raven.

"No," Mr. Raven said, smiling. He turned to Martin. "Go on down to the library and tell Ms. Pendle I sent you." Martin ducked and, keeping the papers from his mother's sight, disappeared out the door.

Mr. Raven walked to a long table at the side of the room. He pulled out a chair and looked at Mrs. Enders. She was much prettier than he remembered. He pulled his smile tighter.

"Have a seat, Mrs. Enders." His voice had suddenly turned thick as yogurt. He cleared his throat, feeling like a bad actor in a TV soap opera. Martin's mother sat and Mr. Raven walked around the table, pulled out a chair, and sat. He looked at her. She isn't as blond as I remember, he thought nervously. She looks great.

"Mrs. Enders," he began.

"Please, Mr. Raven," she interrupted. "Call me Pat."

"Aah . . . Pat," Mr. Raven said, "Please call me Tom." He took a deep breath. "I, ah, I thought we should talk a little bit about Martin and how he's doing this year."

Mrs. Enders looked at him with a crooked smile. Do I need to comb my hair? he wondered, running his fingers through it. He cleared his throat again. "He's having some trouble in school and I'm puzzled."

Martin's mother folded her hands and rested them on the tabletop. Selecting a thoughtful look, Mr. Raven leaned forward. He waited for Mrs. Enders to respond.

"Yes." She looked at Mr. Raven curiously. "I've wondered how he's been doing in school," she said politely. "He doesn't bring home anything from school anymore . . . and I've been having some trouble with him at home." She sat back in her chair as if to say "Your move."

Mr. Raven fiddled with his fingers. "The thing that troubles me is that until a couple of months ago, Martin was one of the best students in class. He was always so . . . helpful and . . . enthusiastic. I've tried everything I can think of and he just seems to get more . . . hostile." Mr. Raven sat back, trying to slow the words coming from his mouth. He took a deep breath. "Martin was fine today, but I think he was worried about our conference." Mr. Raven paused. "Our school records show that you were recently separated and that Martin's father lives in Alaska?" he asked, gingerly.

"Yes." Her smile disappeared. "My husband's business was doing poorly and . . . and everything else started to fall apart."

"Do you think that might have anything to do with Martin's . . . with his attitude problem?"

"Well," she sighed, "of course. If that had happened to either of us when we were his age, we would have had attitude problems too. Martin misses his father. And since Warren and I separated his whole

world has been turned upside down. I know *mine* has."
A frown tugged at the corners of her mouth. "And I'm
sure that I haven't spent enough time with Martin or
with Franny, for that matter. I try. But I've been
working pretty hard, trying to make ends meet." Her
gaze wavered and pain pinched her eyebrows.

"I've told them that it's important for all of us that
I do well in my job and that I go back to school." Pain
squeezed her voice. "It's a strain on all of us." She
looked down at her hands. "I think all of us are still
hurt and confused about the separation . . . and maybe
a little scared."

Mr. Raven's thoughtful look dissolved like sugar
in water. She was describing his own feelings. Hurt.
Confused. Scared.

"Well," he began, swallowing, "I can certainly
understand how all of you feel. I don't know if anybody
ever gets over something like that." He swallowed
again. "At least I haven't."

Mrs. Enders looked up. "You're separated?"

"Divorced." Mr. Raven took a deep breath. "The
papers came through last week. I'm afraid that was
part of the reason I waited so long to talk with you
about Martin. I just didn't have the strength to . . ."
His voice, like a scared rabbit, skittered off into a
bramble of feelings. He wanted to tell Mrs. Enders
how he felt. He wanted to share his pain with her.
He hadn't talked with anybody about his feelings since
he'd moved to Clifton. Not now, he told himself. Not
here. We should be talking about Martin.

He looked into Mrs. Ender's eyes. They looked
back kindly, as if she understood how he felt.

"I've also been wondering about Barney," Mrs. Enders said quietly. "He and Martin used to be such good friends. I don't think they've done anything together since Warren left. Did something happen here at school?"

"I don't know," Mr. Raven said. "But Martin and Barney haven't been getting along very well at all." He looked at Mrs. Enders's mouth, which was pursed in concern. "But I can't say Martin has been getting along with anybody lately."

"Not at home, anyway." Mrs. Enders's smile was sad.

"The other day, I heard something about worms in Barney's soup and I suspect that Martin may have had something to do with that. And today I have a hunch Barney threw Martin's report in a puddle."

Mrs. Enders sighed. "That doesn't sound at all like Martin . . . or Barney. Martin and Barney used to do everything together," she said. "Barney used to bring out the adventure in Martin, make him do things that he wouldn't do on his own."

"I'll see what I can find out," Mr. Raven said. "I think that, especially now, Martin needs a friend he can talk to and who makes him feel good." Don't we all, he thought. Mr. Raven looked at Mrs. Enders and was surprised to feel his heart flop in his chest.

"What can I do to help?" Mrs. Enders asked.

Mr. Raven cleared his throat. "For a start," he said, "I think you should try to get Martin to talk about what he's doing here and what he's feeling. Then I think that Martin should begin completing the reports I assign every week." He smiled. "Last week I assigned a report on animals and Martin decided to write about ravens."

"Ravens?" Mrs. Enders asked, trying not to smile. Mr. Raven nodded. "Excuse me, Tom, but it *is* funny." She chuckled.

Mr. Raven smiled. "He's copying it over right now. But I don't think he would have finished it if I hadn't called this conference. And unfortunately it's the first one he's handed in for at least five weeks." He looked down at his hands and then up again. "I'd be interested in finding out a little more about my family tree . . . or at least the one my family roosted in." He suddenly felt very comfortable with Mrs. Enders. She smiled back at him.

"And I'll look out for his homework . . . " Martin's mother sucked in a breath and turned her head sideways, toward the floor. "What in the world . . . " She hugged her purse and stood up, took a step backward, and knocked over her chair.

Mr. Raven looked at the floor. Mickey waddled to his feet and peered up. He sniffed at Mr. Raven's shoes.

"Mickey!" Mr. Raven bent down and scooped Mickey into his hands. "Mrs. Enders, I mean, Pat, let me introduce you to Mickey." He stroked Mickey's head with his thumb and held him up for Mrs. Enders to see. Mickey nosed Mr. Raven's hands, looking for treats. His naked tail dangled over the edge of Mr. Raven's hands. "He got out of his cage earlier today — while Martin was cleaning it, in fact — and, boy, am I glad he's come out from behind those bookcases!"

"Me too," said Martin's mother. She relaxed the grip on her purse. "I don't normally act silly around pets." She was still breathing hard. "He just startled me. When I was in fifth grade we certainly didn't have *rats*." She smiled weakly. "Except on the playground."

Mr. Raven walked over to Mickey's clean cage, opened the door, and nudged Mickey inside. "Neither did we," he said. "I am sorry he startled you."

"Mr. Raven . . . " Martin stood at the door, looking at Mr. Raven and then at his mother, sizing up the situation. His mother was out of breath. Had they been yelling at each other? Or had Mr. Raven been chasing her around the room? Nah, he thought. That only happens in movies. He turned to Mr. Raven. "Ms. Pendle is leaving and she asked me to come back here."

"Oh," said Mr. Raven.

"But I got my report copied."

That didn't take long, Mr. Raven thought, smiling. "We were just about finished," he said. Mr. Raven looked at Martin's mother. Martin's lucky, he thought. She's a nice woman.

"Correct me if I'm wrong, Mrs. Enders, but I think we decided that the three of us should communicate better with one another." She nodded. "And," Mr. Raven continued, this time to Martin, "I'll give you a week or so to get into the swing of things here at school. If you don't start getting work done and then showing your corrected work to your mother, we'll have another conference to figure something else out. Understand?"

Martin nodded.

"Good," said Mr. Raven. He walked up to Martin and took the report. "I'm glad you got this done," he said in a softer voice. "By the way, we found Mickey" — Mr. Raven smiled at Mrs. Enders — "or Mickey found us."

Martin looked toward Mickey's cage and heard the animal shredding the fresh newspaper he'd put in the cage earlier. "He's OK?" Martin asked.

"I think he had a good vacation," Mr. Raven said, smiling, "and is happy to be home."

"Well, we'd better go now," Martin's mother said. "Thank you, Mr. Raven."

"Tom, please."

"Tom," she said. "I'm sure Martin's performance in school will improve. And let's keep in touch."

"Please," he said. "Let's."

He watched Martin's mother put an arm around the boy's shoulder and walk with him out the door. The click-clack of her heels faded down the hall. He walked to his desk and sat in his teacher's chair. She's had a tough time too, he thought. I wonder what she's studying in school.

Mr. Raven gathered together a stack of papers. He stood up, tucked the papers under one arm, and flung his jacket over his shoulder with the other. He flicked off the light with his elbow and pulled the door shut with his foot.

Not all women are like my ex-wife, he thought as he walked toward the dull light that shone through the double doors at the end of the tunnellike hall. She understands. He threw his shoulder and hip into the door and popped it open. The gray clouds were higher and the rain had stopped. He listened to birds singing in the big, blooming crab apple tree next to the playground.

Mr. Raven strode down the sidewalk. The air was heavy with the smell of crab apple blossoms. A small plane droned like a giant bumblebee, tickling the underside of the clouds. It flew out of sight and the drone faded.

What the heck, he thought. I wonder if she likes Chinese food.

# Chapter 5

———+  +———

"Well?" Franny asked, sitting on the edge of her bed, watching Martin take off his jeans and polo shirt and put on a pair of cutoffs.

"Well, what?" Martin mumbled, zipping the fly.

"You know." Franny sighed, making a flubbing noise with her lips as she breathed out. She picked up Martin's favorite T-shirt from the floor — orange, with "Save the Mosquitoes" on the front and a head-on picture of a mosquito on the back — and handed it to him.

This needs washing, Martin thought as he pulled it on. His head popped out and he opened his eyes, giving Franny a blank look.

"The conference. How'd it go?"

"How should I know," Martin said. He'd tried to figure that out as he and his mother drove home. But his mother had been so lost in thought that she drove by their street.

He'd studied her out of the corner of his eye. For

the first time, Martin noticed little, deep wrinkles underlining her eyes like thin pencil marks emphasizing a word.

Martin jumped when his mother said, "I don't know what your father would do with you." Martin wanted to say, "My father is up in Alaska — probably sleeping with a grizzly bear. He doesn't care." But he didn't open his mouth.

A few minutes later Martin jumped again when she said, "Mr. Raven is a very . . . understanding man." She'd turned to him and her mouth flickered into a grin. "I'm glad you got your report done." She looked ahead and chuckled. "Maybe you could tell me about ravens sometime." She glanced at Martin again. Her smile was gone. "What *will* I do with you, Martin?" She sighed.

Martin's thoughts were interrupted by his sister's voice. "You mean they didn't yell at you or *anything?*" She bounced up and down on her bed. The bed frame squeaked and a book slid off the rumpled sheets and onto the floor.

"Not exactly," Martin said, sitting on his bed and putting on his old sneakers. His big toe stuck out of a hole he'd scraped open by dragging his right foot on the pavement to stop his bike. "They just acted weird when I walked into the room."

"Weird?"

"Yeah. At first I thought they'd been yelling at each other — like Mom and Dad used to." Franny squinted at him. "Then I thought maybe Mr. Raven had been chasing Mom all around the room. She was panting and holding her arm up like this — " Martin demonstrated, holding his left arm up to his heaving chest, his hand patting his heart. "And Mr. Raven was *smiling.*"

"You've got an overactive imagination." Franny crossed her arms. "That doesn't sound at all like Mom *or* Mr. Raven."

"Yeah," Martin admitted, looking down at his feet and wiggling his toe. "She was only trying to get away from Mickey."

"Mickey? What was he doing out?"

"I let him out."

"Oh." She looked at him. "That was dumb."

"If you've got to know *everything*, he got out when I was cleaning his cage," Martin snapped, looking up.

Franny's face split into a grin. "Maybe Mom thinks that Mr. Raven saved her from a rat and now she's madly in love with him."

"With who? With Mickey?" Martin asked.

"With Mr. Raven." Franny began to giggle.

"Sure," Martin said. "Dad's up in Alaska probably falling in love with a moose and Mom's in good ol' Clifton falling madly in love with a raven."

"*Quoth the raven, 'Nevermore!'* " Franny said in a voice that scraped dust from the bottom of her voice box. Laughing, she rolled backward on the bed and flapped her arms like wings. Martin watched his sister and laughed too. *Isn't that the most ridiculous idea in the world? My mother falling in love with Mr. Raven?*

Franny sat up. "That must have been quite a conference." She smiled and gave Martin the once-over. "Looks like you're dressed. Want to help me with dinner tonight?" she asked, getting up.

"Why?" Martin asked. "Where's Mom?"

"She's studying," Franny said. She stepped up to Martin, reaching out to brush the hair from his eyes. He ducked like a turtle and her hand brushed air. "You know, I think she has a chemistry test tomorrow," Franny said, stepping back.

"Yeah." Martin sighed. "Why the hell does she have to study chemistry when she wants to be a gardener?"

"I don't know," Franny said, walking to the door. "Guess it's a requirement."

"What are we having?" Martin stood up.

"We're having hamburgers," she said, turning to look at him.

"Sure. I'll help," Martin said. "I'll get out the buns." He wiggled his butt.

"You dodo," Franny said, walking out the door. "Your buns aren't worth getting out."

Martin frowned as he followed Franny to the kitchen. Sometimes he wanted to throw her out their bedroom window, into the wild roses that grew below.

\* \* \*

As they sat down to dinner, Martin glanced at his mother. She was gazing toward the empty seat his father had always occupied.

"How's the studying going, Mom?" Franny asked, unfolding her napkin and letting it flutter to her lap.

Their mother started and looked at Franny, blinking. "Oh, fine," she said. "I don't think I'm going to do much more than pass the test. Chemistry just isn't my thing." She looked down at the plate. The top half of the bun, sitting on the fat hamburger, was tilted slightly, like a hat. The pickle chip had slid sideways down the patty, looking like an eye patch. "Thanks for making dinner," she said, smiling at Franny and then Martin.

Martin was already eating. His mouth was so full of hamburger that he could barely keep his lips sealed as he chewed. A blob of catsup crawled like a snail from the corner of his mouth, leaving a slimy trail.

"Martin, must you take such large bites?" his mother asked, picking up her hamburger and pressing the bun into the meat. The pickle chip squeezed out and fell onto her plate.

Martin swallowed part of his mouthful, tucking the rest between his cheek and his teeth. "I'm enjoying my food," he said, clenching his jaws. Every time they had hamburgers his mother irritated him by asking him that question. His father used to eat a hamburger in three monstrous bites and his mother never said a word to him. Instead, she always told Martin to take smaller bites, hoping his dad would get the hint. The crawling blob of catsup itched, but he ignored it. He wanted to irritate his mother as much as she irritated him.

His mother put her hamburger on her plate. She picked up her napkin and wiped her chin. "I'm sure pigs enjoy their food, too, but I don't want to eat with one." She stared at Martin. "And while I've got your attention, how can you taste the meat with all that catsup?"

Martin and his mother glared at each other. Martin heard Franny's food mushing around in her mouth as she chewed.

Franny swallowed and cleared her throat. "You know what I read today in the paper?" She put on her cheery, radio-announcer voice. "I read an editorial that said the alarming rate of teenage pregnancies indicates that we, as a country, are not doing a good enough job of teaching our kids about sex." She looked at Martin. Martin's face softened. He turned to Franny and thanked her with his eyes. Now, maybe I can eat in peace, he thought.

"I don't know, Franny," their mother said, taking Franny's bait. She picked up her hamburger and took a bite. "I think everybody today is awfully preoccupied with sex. When I was a kid, for example, movies for teenagers never had locker-room scenes with bouncing boobs and bare bottoms or, heaven forbid, shots of naked people from the front."

"Mo-o-ommm," Franny sang, glancing over at Martin, who was taking a third huge bite of his more-than-half-eaten hamburger. "That's not the point."

"Well, I don't know," their mother said. "I think some of the ads on TV are scandalous. Sometimes I see so much bouncing across the screen I get dizzy."

Hamburger juice oozed out of Martin's mouth as he grinned. Bouncing breasts *were* a big thing on television and in the movies. And Martin didn't think they were so bad.

"What's so funny, Martin?" Franny asked. "Does talking about sex make you nervous?"

Martin looked down at his plate, embarrassed.

Franny turned back to their mother. "If people talked about sex more . . ."

Martin tuned her out and thought of last summer, when he'd heard mewing in the wild roses under their bedroom window. He'd searched under the bushes, which scratched him like cat's claws, and found a little kitten with big, scared eyes. He'd named the skinny thing Chico and fed it milk and kept it in their bedroom, under his bed.

One night, Martin was lying in bed, cuddling Chico on his bare chest. Purring loudly, Chico nuzzled around and, before Martin knew it, began sucking on his left breast, his paws flexing carefully, kneading Martin's skin. It tickled. That's what Mom must have felt when she nursed us, he thought.

Martin's grin disappeared. Not long after that, Chico got distemper and died. His father wouldn't let Martin bury Chico in the backyard. Instead, he put Chico in a garbage sack and threw him in the big can. "It's only a cat," his father had said.

Martin hadn't talked to his dad for a week. And his dad didn't seem to notice.

Martin swallowed his last bite. It stuck halfway down and he swallowed again. "Franny, could you get me some iced tea?" he heard his mother ask. He looked up.

"Sure," Franny said, pushing herself up from her chair.

"Martin," his mother said in a low voice, watching Franny disappear into the kitchen. "I just wanted to say that Mr. Raven and I expect you to do better. We don't know what's gotten into you, but we hope you pick yourself up and stop feeling so sorry for yourself."

"Pick yourself up." Martin frowned. That was one of Dad's favorite phrases. He heard the refrigerator freezer door open and close and the clink of ice falling into a glass.

"We all have enough to worry about without having to worry about how you're doing in school," she continued.

Martin felt himself grow angry. *I'm not worth worrying about?* He opened his mouth to say something nasty — he didn't know what — when Franny walked in carrying a tall glass of iced tea.

"Here you go," she said pleasantly, setting the tea next to her mother's plate. "I was just thinking . . ." She looked at her mother and at Martin, her eyebrows rising like an umbrella opening. "I'm not interrupting anything, am I?" she asked, feigning innocence.

"No," Mrs. Enders said, looking at Martin.

Franny started to sit down when the phone rang. "I'll get it," said Franny, hopping up as if her chair were hot. She caught the phone in the middle of its third ring.

Franny walked back into the room. "It's for you, Mom."

"Who is it?" her mother asked, folding her napkin neatly and putting it beside her plate. She stood up.

"He didn't say."

Their mother walked out of the room.

"What were you talking about?" Franny whispered, picking up her hamburger as she sat down and ripping a bite from it.

"The conference," Martin said, shaking his head. "She told me she had plenty to worry about without having to worry about me."

Franny chewed thoughtfully, watching Martin. "I don't think that's exactly what she meant," she said, swallowing. "But she *does* have enough to worry about. And you have gotten awfully moody lately."

Martin wiped his finger across a blob of catsup on his plate and licked it clean. "You know, it's not like I *enjoy* being moody," he said, looking up. "It's just that everything is so . . . *different* since Dad left. I don't know" — he looked back at his plate — "it's like Mom doesn't even care anymore."

Martin looked up as his mother walked back into the room, thinking and biting a corner of her lower lip.

"Who was it?" Franny asked. She took another bite of hamburger. "A blind date?" she asked through the mouthful. "Or his seeing-eye dog?" She tried not to laugh.

"No," their mother said. She looked at Martin. "It was Mr. Raven."

Oh, no, Martin thought. More trouble. The conference went worse than I thought.

"Boy, Martin, what have you done *now?*" Franny asked.

Martin ignored her. "What did he want?"

"Nothing," Mrs. Enders said, sitting down.

"Nothing?" Franny asked.

"Lay off!" Martin turned toward his sister, his

eyes flashing. She was smiling as she chewed. "You like me to get into trouble, don't you!" Martin turned to his mother.

"Oh, Martin, it's not what you think." His mother looked at him and her eyebrows went up, pulling her forehead into wrinkles like a venetian blind. "You look like you just swallowed a fly!"

She's no better than Franny! Martin fumed.

And then, to Martin's amazement, the wrinkles fell and their mother burst out laughing. "Martin, Martin, Martin."

"You and Mr. Raven must think all of this is pretty funny!" He picked up his napkin and threw it at his plate. "And you too!" He glared at Franny.

Martin stalked from the dining room. "Mar-tin!" his mother called, but he ignored her. He stomped down the hall and into his bedroom, slamming the door shut. If anybody tries to come in, I'll blow up! She wouldn't like it if I laughed at her!

He heard a soft knock at the door. "Martin?" It was his mother. Her voice sounded small, like Franny's. "Martin? May I come in?"

"No!" he said loudly. I don't want to talk to you, he thought. *I wish my father were here!*

"Martin, I'd like to come in and talk with you. I'm sorry I laughed, but you looked so . . . funny."

Martin watched the doorknob twist — like his stomach. The door cracked open. "Martin?" His mother's face peeked at him from behind the door. "Martin, I don't think you understand. . . ." She stepped into the bedroom. She looked at Franny's messy bed and frowned.

"You're right," Martin said. Hamburger burps squeezed up from his knotted stomach. Tears gathered in his eyes. He didn't know exactly why, but he wanted to cry.

"Martin, Mr. Raven didn't call to talk about you." She looked a little embarrassed. "He called to ask me out for dinner."

"What?" Martin's heart skipped a beat.

"I told him I didn't know," his mother said quietly.

*Mr. Raven asked my mother out for dinner? To talk more about me?*

Martin took a deep breath. "You're going out with Mr. Raven?"

"I don't know." She looked at him. "What do you think I should do?"

The door opened wider and Franny strode into the room, her head tipped back and her chin jutting like a plow cutting earth. "Could I get a book, please? I won't stay."

"No!" Martin said. He stood up. "I want to be alone."

"Martin . . ." His mother's face hardened. "I don't think it will take Franny long to . . ."

"No!" Martin said. He stomped his foot on the floor.

Mrs. Enders turned to Franny. "I think Martin should be alone for a while. Let's go do the dishes." She put her arm around Franny's shoulder and they walked out of the room, closing the door behind them.

Martin flopped onto his bed. First she doesn't have enough time to worry about me. And then she and Mr. Raven want to go out to dinner and talk more about me. What is going on? Martin thought angrily.

He scrambled up from his bed and stamped over to his desk. He grabbed a pen and a spiral-ring notebook, threw himself back on his bed, belly down, and wrote as fast as his angry thoughts tumbled through his head.

"Dear Dad," he started. He looked at these two words and crossed them out. "Mr. Enders," he wrote. Martin tried to picture his father reading this letter. Would he be smiling? I'll change that, Martin thought. I'll make him feel as rotten as I feel right now. "You probably don't remember who I am, but I used to be your son when you still lived here. I have a question for you that you probably can't answer because you're so stupid but I'll ask you anyway." He jammed the pen in his mouth.

"If parents can leave each other, why can't kids leave their parents? I want a separation right now from you and from my mother and from Franny too. You get to leave us and sleep with grizzly bears in Alaska and do what you want and I think that it's not fair when I can't do the same thing only I'll go to New Zealand instead of Alaska because I hate your damn guts."

Martin's hand was shaking. But he felt better already. "That's what I think of you and everybody else for that matter."

And then, writing so hard his pen twice poked through the paper, Martin sighed: "Your ex-son and your worst enemy, Martin Patrick Enders the First."

Martin read the letter. I'll mail this to him tomorrow, he thought. Martin closed the notebook, put the pen inside the wire spine, and stuck it under his pillow.

He turned the light off and stretched out on his bed, folded his hands behind his head, and looked out his window into the night. The house was very quiet. He watched a moth crawling on the glass. It looked as if it was crawling on the face of the half moon framed by the window. The moon slowly rose until its sharp point pricked the top of the window. The moth crawled down the length of the moon, crossed over its edge, and walked into the blue-black of space. The moon kept rising, sinking into the window frame deeper and deeper. The moth crawled over a star, blotting it out. Fluttering, it disappeared into the night, leaving the star behind, like a tiny, bright egg.

Martin felt as lost as a moth in space. He'd felt that way the night his father left. He and Franny had cried. His father hadn't. Neither had his mother — until later, when everybody was in bed. He and Franny heard sobs through her bedroom door. Franny closed their door. Their bedroom became stuffy and moist — like tears coming. And the tears had come, making Martin's pillow wet.

Remembering that night, Martin felt tears of confusion bubble up like a hot spring. He shut his eyes and tried to keep them from coming. They squeezed out anyway and Martin wiped them impatiently from his face with the back of his hand.

# Chapter 6

Mr. Raven looked up at a flock of sparrows that covered the branches of a budding oak like dark, fluttering leaves. The birds hushed like students in a classroom as Mr. Raven walked by. He gazed toward the school building, which crouched behind a wall of shrubs, its windows winking catlike as cars drove by.

Why, why, why, why, why? he asked himself. Last night, while he was correcting papers, he jumped up and called Mrs. Enders, just like some hotheaded kid. He shook his head.

Mr. Raven walked up the sidewalk toward a set of double doors. Mr. Clove's face was framed by one of the windows, peering out. What now? he wondered.

The door swung open, like the door at the grocery store. Mr. Clove smiled at Mr. Raven and ushered him inside. "Hello, Tom," he beamed, in his singsong voice, draping an arm over Mr. Raven's shoulder.

The double doors of the school's main entrance

closed, snatching him inside. Fighting an urge to wriggle out from under Mr. Clove's arm, Mr. Raven looked down the long, dim hall, filled with the buzz of fluorescent lights.

"Good morning," Mr. Raven said, looking up at Mr. Clove.

"Yes," Mr. Clove plowed on, "I want us all to get a good start on the day by nipping a little problem in the bud."

What will it be this time? Mr. Raven wondered. Last week Mr. Clove was concerned about body odor. Mr. Raven had wondered how Mr. Clove could smell body odor over the smell of his own coffee breath.

"Your kids are making too many trips to the bathroom," Mr. Clove said, shepherding Mr. Raven down the hall. He took his arm off Mr. Raven's shoulders when they reached Room Five.

How many trips are too many? Mr. Raven wondered, concentrating on the fat, colorful nose that decorated Mr. Clove's face.

"Your class isn't the only one," Mr. Clove continued. "But you can certainly help, Tom." He winked, turned, and bounded down the hall, his heels biting into the shiny linoleum.

"How should I keep them out of the bathroom?" Mr. Raven muttered to the lingering scent of Mr. Clove's after-shave. "Let them pee in their pants?" Sure, Mr. Raven thought, all we need is a supply of diapers. He shook his head as he fumbled for the keys to the classroom. And that's all I need, he sighed — another problem.

*Why did I ask her out for dinner?* The question

came back like a pesky television commercial. Un-locking the door, he walked into the classroom.

Mickey rustled the shredded papers in his cage. The air smelled like the cabinet under Mr. Raven's kitchen sink where little mouse poops gathered like mildewy dill seeds.

Mr. Raven frowned at the classroom clock. *Five minutes to blast-off.* His stomach yawned and stretched. *Better get some assignments on the board.* His heart thumped.

He grabbed a piece of chalk, making white chips fly as he wrote the morning's schedule on the board.

The bell rang and kids spilled in from the hall like water from a busted water main. Mr. Raven rested the chalk on the tray, turned, and leaned back. This is the best show in town, he thought, watching Harold sit at his desk and stick his leg out to trip Carrie. Without missing a beat, Carrie hopped over his leg, turned her head, and stuck out her tongue at Harold — all at the same time. Mr. Raven looked up and saw Martin shamble in behind everybody else.

"Good morning, Martin," Mr. Raven said.

Martin looked at him, his eyes blank. "Good morning," he mumbled.

He looks quite a bit like his mother, Mr. Raven thought, watching Martin. Same hair. Same chin.

Mr. Raven looked around the classroom and felt the energy of the kids fill him up, like electricity re-charging a battery. He was ready for the day.

* * *

From his desk, Mr. Raven watched his students work on math assignments, their pencils scritching like

Mickey in his cage. Mr. Raven's gaze stopped at Martin. Martin was staring at his paper, doing nothing. He walked to Martin's desk. "How are the fractions going?" Mr. Raven asked, dropping to one knee and looking at the lined paper next to Martin's open math book. The paper was blank except for eraser smudges and Martin's name on top.

"Fine," Martin mumbled.

"These are a little tricky at first," Mr. Raven observed. "Why don't we work on this first problem together?" He studied Martin. "Then you can do the rest by yourself." Mr. Raven took the pencil from Martin's hand. "Now," said Mr. Raven, clearing his throat, "we want to divide four-fifths by five-eights."

Martin stared glumly at the paper. He hated not knowing what to do.

"We write the problem down like this . . ." Mr. Raven tried to write as neatly as he told his students to write. Even so, his four looked like a nine. He marked over it several times to make it clear.

"Now, what is the first thing we should do with these fractions?" Mr. Raven asked.

"Invert and multiply?" Martin guessed, scrunching up his face.

"That's right!" Mr. Raven was pleased that Martin knew. "We invert five-eighths . . . like this and . . ." A sweet odor wafted past them and Mr. Raven sniffed the air as he wrote. " . . . and that means we do what to the divided-by sign?" That smells like the cherry cough drops we used to eat secretly in class when I was in fifth grade, Mr. Raven thought.

"You change it to a multiplication sign?" Martin asked, struggling not to show his excitement.

"Right!" Mr. Raven said. He tried to concentrate on the fraction problem but the odor made him think of the time a teacher accused him of sucking on a cherry cough drop. Instead of spitting out the evidence, he'd swallowed it. The cough drop had stuck in his chest like a button for a long time.

Mr. Raven blinked. "Now, where were we? Ah yes. We have a multiplication problem instead of a division problem," he said. The cherry smell was stronger now. "You multiply the numerators together — " Mr. Raven wrote a twenty-four and underscored it with a line. ". . . and then you multiply the denominators together . . ."

"That's wrong," Martin mumbled, feeling a rush of pride. He caught himself before he smiled.

Mr. Raven sniffed the air again. He heard giggling. "Ah . . . what, Martin?" He heard another giggle and then a cough, as if someone had swallowed wrong. What's going on? Mr. Raven asked himself.

"That's wrong," Martin repeated. "It should be thirty-two." He tried to sound bored.

Mr. Raven looked at the paper, confused. "Ah, four times eight is . . ." he mumbled, and then smiled. "Hey, Martin, you're right. Why don't you fix that up?" He handed Martin the pencil and turned quickly to look behind him.

From the corner of his eye, he saw Barney dip his head to his desk. Barney tried to contain his coughing but, instead, exploded into a fit and banged his forehead onto his desktop.

"Excuse me," Mr. Raven said to Martin. He walked toward Barney, whose forehead was pressed against his desk as he coughed.

"Are you all right, Barney?" Mr. Raven knelt beside Barney's desk. The smell of cherry and alcohol fogged from Barney's mouth as he coughed. Mr. Raven saw a tiny uncapped medicine-type bottle in Barney's right hand. Mr. Raven reached for the bottle, but Barney, still coughing, pulled it away and put his hand under his desk.

"Barney, what *is* that?" The classroom was so still Mr. Raven heard Mickey trotting in his squeaky exercise wheel. "Barney, I'd like to see what you have in your hand."

Tears streaming down his face, Barney tried not to cough. His voice shook. "Nothing." He swallowed, gagged, and exploded into more coughing.

"I'd like to see what you have in your hand," Mr. Raven repeated firmly.

Barney slowly brought up his shaking hand and handed the little bottle to Mr. Raven. Mr. Raven raised the bottle to his nose and smelled. His nose tingled and he blinked. Unmistakable. He was smelling cherry liqueur.

Mr. Raven stared at Barney, growing angry.

"The lid?" he demanded. Barney reached into his pocket and pulled it out.

Mr. Raven stared at Barney's tearing eyes. "I'd like you to go to Mr. Clove's office. Now." Each word hung in the air. Mr. Raven stood up. He looked around the room. Everybody was staring at him.

"Class," he said, "finish your math assignments." The breeze in his voice cut through the stillness in the room. The kids kept staring. "Now!" Mr. Raven barked. The kids dove into their work.

Mr. Raven watched Barney stand up and walk unsteadily out the door. Mr. Raven turned and walked to his desk. He eased into his chair, leaned back, and pulled out the middle drawer. Mr. Raven tightened the lid and stuck the bottle behind the trays that held paper clips and rubber bands and loose change for the soda machine in the teachers' lounge. As he pushed the drawer in, the bottle rolled and came to a stop. Mr. Raven's stomach felt weak.

I've read about kids in big cities who drink in school, he thought. But things like this are not supposed to happen in towns like Clifton. Why? Mr. Raven asked. Why would Barney do something like that? He remembered Mrs. Enders's comment from the conference: "Barney used to bring out the adventure in Martin," she'd said. Well, Mr. Raven thought, leaning back in his chair, that's one adventure Martin would have talked Barney out of.

Mr. Raven watched the pie-shaped slice of time on the classroom clock grow five minutes larger. He stood up and surveyed the classroom. Martin was still staring at his paper.

Mr. Raven walked up to Martin. "How are the fractions going?" The friendliness was gone from his voice. He knelt to look at Martin's paper. The only marks he saw were the ones he'd made.

"Fine," Martin mumbled.

Mr. Raven swallowed hard and breathed deeply. Patience, he said to himself. Patience.

Mr. Raven took the pencil from Martin's hand. "Let's start by changing this twenty-four to thirty-two . . ." He began erasing the twenty-four and tore a triangular hole in the paper. "Martin, you should have another pencil. Let me lend you one." He stood up and turned toward his desk. Out of the corner of his eye he saw Mr. Clove standing in the doorway, a grim look on his face.

"Martin," Mr. Raven said, looking down at Martin. "Go get a pencil out of the middle drawer of my desk. I'll be with you in a minute." Mr. Raven put the pencil stub on Martin's desk. As he walked toward the door, Mr. Clove stepped into the hall shadows.

Dipping his head slightly, Mr. Raven walked toward the door as if he were walking into a spraying hose.

"Mr. Raven," Mr. Clove began the moment Mr. Raven stepped into the hall, "I have a very sorry little boy in my office right now who smells like he's been dipping into the communion wine, so to speak." Mr. Clove's eyes were hard. They didn't match his toothy smile.

"Yes," Mr. Raven said, "I caught him with a little bottle of cherry liqueur during math and I thought you should handle it."

"It's taken care of," Mr. Clove said. "I don't think you'll be having problems like that from Barney in the future. He claims he didn't bring it to school but he won't tell me who did." Mr. Clove's face clouded over. "I think we should have a talk after school about stopping these things in class before they happen. Never," Clove's voice was firm, "never have I had a student in this school caught in class with anything stronger than root beer. And . . . " Mr. Raven knew what was coming — it was one of Mr. Clove's favorite phrases. " . . . I've been at this school for fifteen years."

Mr. Raven blinked. He wasn't used to being talked to as if he were a kid. He didn't like it when he *was* a kid and he especially didn't like it now that he was an adult.

"Mr. Clove," he said, not knowing what was going to come out of his mouth, but unable to contain his frustration, "I am very sorry that anything like that happened in my class. But I'm sure these things happen to the best of teachers. I *am* in control of that class and they *are* learning."

Mr. Clove's face hardened. "We'll discuss this after school," he said. "And please bring that little bottle with you." He turned on his heels and walked down the hall. He stopped and turned. "I'll send Barney back to class after he's had a chance to clean up. But I've taken away his recesses for the next week."

Great, Mr. Raven thought. Who is Mr. Clove punishing, anyway — me or Barney? Now I'll have to stay in the classroom with him. Without another word, Mr. Raven turned and walked back into the class room. That frosts me, he thought. That really frosts my cup cakes.

The kids were quiet. He walked up to Martin and looked down at Martin's paper. Martin had finished the first problem and was starting the second.

"I knew you could do that," Mr. Raven said drily.

"But it's time to start reading. I'd like you to come in during the noon recess and finish up today's assignment."

As the morning wore on, Mr. Raven felt more and more like a flashlight growing dimmer and dimmer. By lunchtime, his mood was fading into darkness. What if Mr. Clove fires me? he asked himself. What if he does, he answered. Maybe I'll tell him I quit.

He trudged to the teachers' lounge and ate quietly so that he could be in the classroom before Barney arrived for the lunch recess. As he ate, he noticed that everybody else's lunch looked much better than his. The cigarette smoke was overpowering the taste of his sandwich's jelly.

"Tom." He looked up at Mrs. Roar. She was smoking.

"Some of the kids in my class told me that Martin put some worms in Barney's soup the other day. Is that true?"

"Well," he said, swallowing a lump of tasteless sandwich, "I don't know."

"I just couldn't believe a word of it. Why, last year, when they were in my class, they were inseparable." She inhaled deeply. "They were such good friends," she said, smoke pouring from her nose and mouth.

Mr. Raven stood up, sticking his half-eaten banana back into his brown paper sack.

"Something wrong, Tom?" Smoke puffed out of Mrs. Roar's mouth with each word. She took another drag and slowly exhaled.

"No," Mr. Raven sighed. "I just have to get back to work."

"Don't work too hard," Mrs. Roar said as Mr. Raven walked out of the lounge. The last word was cut short as the door clicked shut behind him.

Mr. Raven was surprised when he walked into the room to see Martin already at his desk, working on his math assignment. Noon recess hadn't begun yet.

"Martin, how did you get in here?" he asked, walking to Martin's desk.

"I told Ms. Pendle that you wanted me to come in early to work on fractions," Martin said.

Mr. Raven looked down at the papers on Martin's desk. "How are you doing?" He saw that Martin was working on problem five.

"OK," Martin said frowning.

"Fractions aren't so bad when you learn the tricks," Mr. Raven said. "Let me know if you run into any difficulty." He turned and walked to his desk.

Just as he sat down, Barney walked in, his hands jammed into the pockets of his jeans, his shoulders hunched, frowning at his feet. He shuffled toward his desk and, without taking his hands out of his pockets, slumped into his seat. He glared at Martin and pinched his nostrils together.

"Hello, Barney," Mr. Raven said sternly. "I expect you to read. Do you have a book?"

"No," Barney mumbled, not taking his eyes off Martin.

"Look at me when I talk to you," Mr. Raven said

angrily. Barney turned his head and looked at Mr. Raven, fear and anger glinting in his eyes.

"I am very disappointed in you, Barney," Mr. Raven continued. "I have never had something like this happen in class. I don't know how you thought you could get away with that stunt. I'm not stupid." Mr. Raven paused for a moment to catch his breath. I don't want to say something I'll regret, he told himself. Calm down. Calm down.

"Well," Mr. Raven said, "if you don't have a book, I have one that you might find interesting." He reached over a pile of papers on his desk and grabbed a dog-eared hard-bound book. "*The Hobbit*," he said, standing up and walking over to Barney's desk. He handed the book to Barney. "This book is probably as old as you are."

Without saying a word, Barney drew one hand out of its pocket and took the book. He reluctantly opened it to the first chapter.

"I just love the way it begins." Mr. Raven's mind and body relaxed as he closed his eyes, tilted his head back, and cleared his throat. " 'In a hole in the ground there lived a hobbit. Not a nasty, dirty, wet hole, filled with the ends of worms and an oozy smell, nor yet a dry, bare, sandy hole with nothing in it to sit down on or to eat: it was a hobbit-hole, and that means comfort.' " He opened his eyes and looked at Barney. "Did I get that right?" he asked.

Barney nodded, his eyes wide.

"I think I've read that book almost every year since I was your age," said Mr. Raven. "It starts out

81

slow, but give it a try. I think you'll like it." He walked
back to his desk. I wish I were in Middle Earth, he
thought as he sat down, talking to Gandalf or Bilbo
Baggins or singing with elves.

Mr. Raven stared at a pile of uncorrected papers.
I'm not in the mood, he thought, looking up. Martin
was writing numbers down as fast as he could. And
Barney was reading *The Hobbit*, a frown creasing his
forehead and a smile tickling the corners of his mouth.

Those two should be friends, Mr. Raven thought.
They complement each other.

Martin snapped his book shut, sighed, and got
up. He walked to Mr. Raven's desk and handed Mr.
Raven his math assignment. He avoided Mr. Raven's
eyes.

"Thanks," Mr. Raven said. "I'd like you to read
until recess is over."

* * *

The last thing for the day was a science exercise
in which groups of students each got a box of loose cat
bones and had to arrange them on a piece of black felt,
like a jigsaw puzzle. When the desks were arranged
in clumps and the kids were busy, Mr. Raven retreated
to his desk to correct the morning's math papers.

He pulled the stack toward him and opened the
middle drawer of the desk to get a correcting pen.

The pens and pencils, usually in the long tray in
the front, were scattered over the back of the drawer.
The loose change he kept in a corner tray was gone.
Mr. Raven frowned as he pulled the drawer out until
it touched his stomach. He looked at the rulers and

scissors and slips of paper strewn among the pencils
and pens and suddenly noticed that the bottle of cherry
liqueur was not there.

Oh no, he thought, suddenly angry. Mr. Clove
will be furious if I don't show up with that bottle after
school.

He looked at Martin, who was holding the cat's
skull up to the light and examining it. Mr. Raven didn't
like what he was thinking. But Martin had been in the
room alone at noon, Mr. Raven thought grimly. And
when Mr. Clove appeared during math, I told him to
get a pencil from my desk. Those two things made
Martin the prime suspect.

Mr. Raven tried to look calm, but he could feel
the pressure of anger building. I can't accuse Martin
of anything without proof, he reasoned. And, to get
proof, I'll have a little desk-cleaning session after science, he decided.

After the bones had been picked up, Mr. Raven
made his announcement.

"I have a special treat for you this afternoon." He
paused dramatically. "I've noticed that some of your
desks are in really bad shape. Before we go home, I
want each of you to clean your desk." The class groaned.
"When your desk is clean, raise your hand and I'll
come inspect it. Barney," he said, looking at Barney,
"would you go across the hall and borrow a waste
basket from Mrs. Roar?"

As papers began to fly, Mr. Raven sidled over
toward Martin's desk. Martin was calmly emptying the
contents of his desk onto his chair, separating the pa-

pers from the books. Mr. Raven peered casually into Martin's desk, but didn't see the little bottle.

Martin looked up quizzically. Mr. Raven smiled back. This was a silly idea, Mr. Raven thought as he walked down the row, looking at the desks on either side. Martin could have put it in his pocket. In Harold's desk he saw a big wad of chewed gum that was partly wrapped up in a sheet of lined paper. I'll have to talk with him about that tomorrow, he thought.

He got to Barney's desk just as Barney walked up with the borrowed waste basket. "Thanks, Barney," he said as the boy put it down and opened his desk. Mr. Raven froze. Right on top, nestled between Barney's math and reading books, was the bottle. Mr. Raven pulled it out and shook it. The bottle was empty.

"Barney," he said softly, "do you have any idea how this got into your desk?"

Barney's jaw dropped. "No," he whispered.

Mr. Raven turned and walked toward Martin, who was putting things back in his desk.

"Martin," he said softly, dropping to one knee next to Martin. He held out the bottle. "This was in Barney's desk." Martin's eyes grew large. "Was anybody here when you came to the room after lunch?"

Martin was too surprised to say anything. He had bumped into Clyde in the hallway. But Martin hadn't seen him in the room.

"No," Martin said.

Sighing, Mr. Raven stood up. He walked back to Barney. "Barney," he said. "I think we should have a little talk this afternoon. After school."

"But I didn't do anything!" Barney said loudly, looking at Martin, pain on his face. Martin returned his stare, tight-lipped. "I didn't do anything!"

"I didn't say that you did," Mr. Raven replied. "I just think that we should have a little talk."

Mr. Raven stuck the bottle in his pocket as he walked to his desk. Whoever took this from my desk is making a fool out of me, he thought sadly.

# Chapter 7

"Mom!" Franny stared as her mother walked into the living room, cinching a thin belt that gathered her skirt around her waist. "You're going to class in that?"

Mrs. Enders tucked the belt's end into a loop. "Do I look funny?" she asked.

Franny put down her book and sat up in the sofa. "That's not what I meant," she said. "You don't normally wear a dress for chemistry class, that's all." She looked down at the black pumps her mother was wearing. "Where *are* you going?"

Her mother studied her. "I can't keep anything secret from you, can I?" she said, settling into a chair opposite the couch and crossing her legs. "Well, I was invited out for dinner and I decided to skip chemistry and go."

Franny threw herself back into the sofa and rested her head in her cupped hands. Her elbows pointed up and out like wings. "I thought so," she said smugly.

"Oh, you did, did you?" Mrs. Enders said. "And what gave me away?"

"Well, for one thing," Franny said, flapping her elbows back and forth, "you're all dressed up. For another, you're late for class. For another, you don't have your books with you. For another, you haven't eaten anything to help you get through the evening. For another — "

"That's OK, Franny," Mrs. Enders laughed.

"But the biggest thing that gave you away is you seem happy to be going and *that's* not at all like you going to chemistry class."

Mrs. Enders chuckled. "I suppose you know who I'm going to eat dinner with?"

"I think I know who you're *not* going with." Franny turned so that her right shoulder was leveled at her mother. She rested her left elbow on the back of the sofa, positioning herself like a television talk-show host, and aimed her gaze over the round of her shoulder. "I don't think you're going with that Mr. Zucker, because he tried to invite himself over for the night."

"Franny!" Mrs. Enders said, embarrassed. "Of course not."

"And I don't think you're going with that turkey who smelled like he took a bath in after-shave and combed hair over his bald spot." Franny smiled knowingly. "And I don't think that you're going with Mr. Raven, even though he asked you the other night."

"You don't?"

Franny wrinkled her nose at her mother. "Mom, Mr. Raven happens to be Martin's teacher."

"So?" Mrs. Enders uncrossed her legs and placed her feet squarely on the floor.

"Well, how would you feel if your teacher started dating *your* mother?"

Mrs. Enders looked at the floor. "Hmm," she breathed softly. "Hmm. If I had any questions about homework, I'd know who to ask." She looked up at Franny, her eyes encouraging Franny to laugh.

"Mom." Franny grimaced.

"You've got a point," Mrs. Enders said, feebly. "I don't know how I'd feel, but I don't think I'd be too happy."

"So that's who you're going with," Franny said grimly, curling her legs underneath herself.

"Yes." Mrs. Enders grabbed the arms of the chair and hoisted herself up. "That's who I'm going with. Maybe we shouldn't tell Martin."

Franny nodded.

"And I'm late."

"Like always." Franny's smile tightened. "Mom," she said, picking up her book and getting up from the couch. "I know that Mr. Raven is a nice man. But I don't think you two should get involved."

Mrs. Enders frowned as she put on her coat. "Trust me. I'm old enough to take care of myself."

"I'm not worried about you. I'm worried about Martin." Franny watched her mother button her coat. "Well, the least you can do is be home by ten o'clock at the latest," she sighed.

"Yes, dear," Mrs. Enders said, smiling. "And I'd like you in bed by nine."

"I can't," Franny said. Her smile disappeared. "If I'm in bed by nine, I won't know if you got home by ten."

"That's right." Mrs. Enders's eyes twinkled. "Franny, where's Martin?"

"I don't know. He's probably in our bedroom sulking."

"Well, tell him that he's to go to bed by nine too and that both of you may read for a half hour before lights out. Oh," she said, turning from the front door, "there are TV dinners in the freezer. Bye."

"Bye," Franny said, turning toward the kitchen. "Have a good time."

The door thunked shut.

"I'm sure she will."

Startled, Franny turned in midstep toward the hall. "Martin! Were you eavesdropping?"

"No," Martin said. "Just listening." He walked out of the shadow, toward the kitchen. "It's a free country, isn't it?" He was trying not to let shock and hurt echo in the hollowness he felt inside. His mother had decided to go out with Mr. Raven after all. And she hadn't told him.

*　*　*

"I'm glad that you could get away tonight, Pat," Mr. Raven said, over the clinking of plates, people talking, and Oriental-style music. Clouds of spicy smells engulfed them when waiters walked by.

"Well," Mrs. Enders said, looking at a dark Chinese painting across the room, "I didn't tell Martin that I was going out to dinner. In fact, he thinks that I'm off to my chemistry class at the university extension."

"You're missing chemistry to be here tonight?" Mr. Raven curled his legs around his chair legs. "If I'd known, I would have suggested another . . ."

"That's all right," Mrs. Enders smiled. "There's not much chemistry between me and chemistry."

Mr. Raven tried to think of something clever to say in return. Before he could say anything, she said, "You know, when you called the other night, he wasn't very excited about the idea of my going out with you."

"Oh?" Mr. Raven looked at his place mat. "I almost didn't call because I didn't know what Martin would think." He looked up. "I don't think I would have been very happy. But then" — he grinned — "it probably would have depended on the teacher."

"I don't want Martin to feel as if I'm talking behind his back," Mrs. Enders said, "but I want to know how things went today."

"Better," Mr. Raven said. "I think that Martin was trying today. And I think he surprised himself by being better at fractions than he thought he would be."

"That's a relief," Mrs. Enders said. "I've thought about what we discussed during the conference, and I think I've been trying to cope so much with Warren's . . . he's my husband . . . with his leaving I haven't been able to help Martin and Franny cope. Sometimes I get the feeling that Martin would much rather be up in Alaska with his father than with me," she said. "Other times, Martin seems so angry at his father. I don't want Martin to hate his father, but I have a hard time trying to tell Martin that his father is remarkable. *I* have a hard time telling myself that."

Mr. Raven nodded.

"Did you have any kids?" Mrs. Enders asked.

"No."

Mrs. Enders slipped her chopsticks out of their paper sleeve. "Even though Franny and Martin don't get all the attention they need, I don't know how I could have kept on without them."

"Are you going to get a divorce?" Mr. Raven asked.

"I hope it all comes through soon," Mrs. Enders said. "The lawyer keeps telling me that we're just waiting for Warren to sign the last batch of papers."

"Getting divorced takes a lot more effort than getting married, that's for sure," Mr. Raven said. He looked up from the tablecloth. "Why did you separate?"

"Well," Mrs. Enders frowned, "Warren . . ." She split her chopsticks apart. "He felt, I don't know, trapped . . . restless. His business was falling apart. He wanted to start again, fresh. He wanted to go someplace exciting, where he could live off the land." She looked up at Mr. Raven. "I don't know if *he* knows exactly why he left. He was always impatient with people who asked too many questions . . . who didn't just *do* what they wanted." She looked at her chopsticks. "He was always impatient with people like me . . . and like Martin."

Mr. Raven nodded. "So he just took off?"

"He gave me a choice. Move with him up to Alaska and start our lives over or stay here with what little we owned. I chose to stay."

"That must have been tough," Mr. Raven said lamely.

"Yes," Mrs. Enders said, rubbing the chopsticks together. "It was especially tough because Warren was flat broke and I didn't make enough money to keep up our house payments or feed and clothe the kids." She grinned. "I think Warren thought I would be up in Alaska after a month, begging him to take us in." Her forehead wrinkled. "It's been hard, but we're getting along." She put down the chopsticks and creased the upper left corner of her place mat. "Why did you get divorced?" she asked, looking up.

The waitress walked up with their food and wine. They didn't say anything while she set steaming plates on the table and poured the wine.

Mr. Raven picked up his chopsticks. "There were a lot of reasons," he said, trying not to drop the food dangling from his chopsticks. "I think that we basically got married for the wrong reasons."

Mrs. Enders nodded as she brought a glob of vegetables to her mouth. Everything fell off just before she could pop it into her mouth.

"I guess that I've learned that you just can't be happy being with somebody until you're happy being with yourself. We got married so young I don't think I knew who I was or if I even liked myself."

"I've certainly learned a lot about myself since Warren left," Mrs. Enders said thoughtfully. "And some of it hasn't been very pleasant to find out."

Mr. Raven pinched some food in his chopsticks and dipped his head toward his plate so that nothing would fall off. "Like a lot of people," he said, sitting up, "we tried to fix everything up by having a kid. We thought that a baby would bring us closer together."

Mrs. Enders nodded.

"We never found out if it would work for us, though," Mr. Raven said. "We tried, but as time went on I noticed that Phoebe was getting more and more distant. Noncommunicative. We'd stopped trying to have a baby. And then one day she told me she'd been to the doctor." Mr. Raven took a bite of shrimp. "She didn't look happy, so I assumed everything was negative again." He looked at Mrs. Enders and she nodded. Should I be telling her this? he wondered. I haven't talked about this with anybody for a long time.

Mr. Raven's lower lip quivered and he cleared his throat. I guess I can't turn back now, he thought. The music seemed very loud and he couldn't hear people talking. He glanced around. Nobody was staring. He heard a man laugh, and the murmur of voices grew, as if somebody had turned up the volume. He faced Mrs. Enders. "Instead, she told me that she was pregnant but that I wasn't the father. That she'd met a young man in law school — she was working in the library. This *kid* was the father."

Mrs. Enders put down her chopsticks and reached across the table. "That's horrible, Tom." He put his hand on hers and squeezed.

Mr. Raven looked down at his food. "She asked me if I thought she should get an abortion. I told her that I would hate for a baby to be killed on my account and that she should work that out with her . . . lover."

"What did she do?" Mrs. Enders's voice was small.

"I moved out and the boy moved in. They had the kid five months ago." He let go of her hand and picked up his chopsticks. "They're planning to get married . . . sometime."

Mrs. Enders picked up her chopsticks and they ate in silence for several minutes.

"Martin said that you had just moved from somewhere."

"Yes." Mr. Raven tried to sound more upbeat. He pecked at his food with the beaklike chopsticks. "I just couldn't stay in the same town with them. And, frankly, I don't think they'll be able to stay there much longer either. Small towns aren't very forgiving."

* * *

Martin couldn't sleep. He punched his pillow into different shapes, trying to make a nest for his head. He lay on his back and stared unblinking at the ceiling until it seemed to sink toward him. He lay on his stomach until he could hear his heart beating through the mattress. He lay on his side until he got a crick in his neck.

Martin listened to the soft breathing of his sister across the room. How can she sleep knowing that Mom is with Mr. Raven right now? he thought angrily. Doesn't she care?

Franny sucked in sharply and rolled over on her side, facing the opposite wall. In the morning I'll tell her that she was hugging and kissing her pillow in her sleep, Martin decided. That she was softly calling out for Christopher, the heartthrob of sixth grade. Maybe I can make her blush.

I hope Mom and Mr. Raven are having a rotten time, Martin thought, turning onto his side and closing his eyes. Sleep sheep, sleep sheep, sleep sheep, sleep, he said over and over. But an image of Mr. Raven and his mother walking toward him, hand in hand, flashed through his brain. Martin opened his eyes quickly and flopped onto his back with a sigh.

It's hot in here, Martin thought crossly. He kicked his covers to the foot of his bed and spread his arms and legs across the width of the bed. Martin lay quietly, wondering what it would be like to be stretched like this, naked, staked to a red anthill in the desert. He pictured himself surrounded by cloaked, shadowy men laughing as ants crawled over him in the blazing sun. That's what I'd like to do to Mr. Raven, he thought.

An itch suddenly pricked at his thigh and Martin sat up quickly to scratch. I'm still hot, he thought miserably. Reaching behind his shoulders, he pulled off his pajama top and threw it on the floor by his bed. I'd take off my bottoms, too, if I had my own room, he thought.

He looked over at Franny. What's to stop me from taking them off? he asked himself. He pushed his bottoms off and kicked them toward the blankets. Martin lay back on his bed. Just me and my bawd-y, he sang to himself. The air of the room felt like a cool sheet against his skin. Just me and my bawd-y.

Franny grunted and turned over, facing Martin, her eyes closed. Martin sat up like a pocketknife snapping shut and grabbed for the pajama bottoms at his feet. He jammed his feet into them and yanked up until the elastic band encircled his chest. I hate sharing this room with her, he though bitterly. She won't even let me open the bedroom window.

If Dad's business hadn't been so bad, if he hadn't fought with Mom, if he hadn't moved to Alaska — if, if, if, if, if — we would be adding my bedroom to our house this spring, he thought, reaching over the bed and grabbing his pajama tops. Dad promised.

If I had my own room I could sleep naked if I wanted. But then I wouldn't even need to, he thought, pulling the tops over his head and shooting his arms through the sleeves. I could open the window and let the breeze through.

Martin looked at Franny. Why not open the window? he thought. She'll never know. And, in the morning, when she finds out, it will be too late.

Quietly, Martin got out of bed and stealthily walked toward the window. He looked out, over the top of the wild rose bush under the window. He lifted the window and felt cool air seep into the room. Suddenly two shafts of blinding light swung onto him as a car pulled into their driveway. He dropped to the floor and slowly poked his head above the window sill.

The headlights darkened and the motor stopped. The door swung open and Martin watched his mother stand up behind it. She reached inside, pulled out her purse, and closed the door.

Martin watched her walk slowly up the driveway until she disappeared around the corner of the house. He held his breath and listened for the back door to open and close. When he heard his mother walk through the kitchen, he scurried to his bed, jumped in, pulled the covers to his chin, and faced Franny's bed. He tried to control his breathing.

Her footsteps grew louder. Martin cracked his eyelids open and watched the door move. His mother looked inside, first at Franny and then at Martin. She gazed across the room to the window and, opening the door wider, she stepped into the bedroom. Walking on tiptoe, to keep her heels from hammering the floor, she crossed the room and closed the window. She turned and tiptoed to Franny's bed, stooping to kiss Franny lightly on the forehead and to pull the covers over Franny's shoulders. I hope she doesn't do that to me, Martin thought. But he closed his eyes tightly when he saw her turn and look at him.

He heard her tiptoe to his bed. He felt the disturbed air as she bent toward him. He smelled the sweetness of wine on her breath as she touched her lips to his forehead.

Yuck, Martin thought, trying not to cringe. Mr. Raven might have been kissing those lips all evening. I might have Mr. Raven germs on my forehead. Martin's body tensed as he listened to his mother cross the room and close the door quietly behind her.

His hand shot up from under his blankets and his fist vigorously rubbed the spot where his mother had kissed him.

# Chapter 8

"Mar-tin," Franny whispered into Martin's ear.

He drew the blankets tighter around his head. Why is she whispering? Martin grumped. Is she afraid she'll wake me up?

"Mar-tin." She whispered more softly and gently shook his shoulder.

"Martin!" she said sharply, reaching over him and, just as he was breathing in, burying his face in a feather duster. He blinked. Grit scoured his eyes.

"Arrg!" Martin grunted. His nose filled with the smell of spider webs and dust. He threw off his blankets and grabbed for the duster. He grabbed too close and scratched the side of his nose with his thumbnail. He grabbed again.

Martin scrambled upright, but Franny had already flown out of the room.

Stomping into the kitchen, Martin threw the feather duster onto the table.

"Where do you want it?" His voice was as gritty as the dust on his lips. He tried not to lick them.

"My left arm," Franny said pleasantly, sitting down.

"How much?"

"Forty units."

Martin prepared the syringe. And, before he could stop himself, he jabbed the needle into her arm harder than he'd ever jabbed before.

"Mar-tin!" Franny squeaked. Tears beaded in the outside corners of her eyes. "That hurt!" She rubbed the spot on her arm where Martin had just yanked out the needle.

Martin stared at the needle, horrified. "I'm sorry," he muttered. He turned his head so that he couldn't see Franny's face. Trying to sound gruff, he asked, "Why don't you learn to give your own shots?" His insides felt mushy.

"Dad would never have done something like that." Franny's mouth shook.

"No." Martin looked at Franny, surprised. I could never do anything like my father, he thought angrily. Is she telling me I'm not as good as Dad? "No. He just took off and left us here. That's all."

Franny winced, as if Martin had jabbed her again. Don't look at me that way, he wanted to say. *I* didn't take off. *He* did.

"Did Mom come back last night?" Martin asked sarcastically. "Or did she take off too?"

"Martin!"

Franny and Martin turned toward the kitchen door. Their mother was buttoning the top button of her blouse.

"You may or may not be pleased to know that I'm still here and that I don't like you to talk that way." Mrs. Enders walked briskly toward Martin, tucking her blouse more tightly into her skirt. "You'd better get dressed for school. You're late," she said sharply.

Martin slapped the syringe on the kitchen table. "Did you have a good time last night?" he asked. The refrigerator hum echoed in his head.

"Yes," she said quietly.

"Why didn't you tell me!" he shouted as he stormed out of the kitchen before his mother could answer and slammed the bedroom door.

I *bet* they had a good time last night, he thought — talking about me. I suppose they talked about me and then went out to some vacant lot and necked, Martin thought, taking off his pajamas and rummaging around in his dresser.

Franny opened the door and stood with her hands on her hips. "I hope Mom is right," she said, "that it's just a stage you're going through."

"Why the hell don't you knock before you come in?" Martin grabbed a T-shirt and wrapped it around his waist. It didn't go all the way around. "I don't like you marching in here when I don't have any clothes on. Or," he pursed his lips and tipped his head back and forth with every other word, "do you get your jollies staring at naked boys?" He swung his hips back and forth and the T-shirt slipped out of his fingers and dropped to the floor. He covered his front with one hand and picked it up with the other.

"You're really weird, Martin," Franny said, walking to her desk and picking up a stack of books. "You're *just* a boy," she said. "And you're *not* exactly a *hunk.*"

Martin glared at his sister. He raised the T-shirt and swung it around his head as he stomped toward her.

"Oh, my." Franny pointed to Martin's crotch. "Is it a boy or a girl?"

Martin threw his arm down. The T-shirt fluttered, grabbed, and whipped around Franny's neck and shoulder like a scarf.

Franny pulled the T-shirt off her shoulder with her thumb and forefinger. She wrinkled her nose and scrunched up her face. "Oh, it smells like a boy," she said. Letting the T-shirt drop to the floor, she glided out of the room.

What does she know? Martin fumed. He hated getting into fights with his sister. He always lost. Martin scooped the T-shirt from the floor.

It's not a stage *I'm* going through, Martin thought as he dressed. My parents are the ones going through some kind of stage. First my father leaves and then my mother starts to go out with my teacher. I'm probably the most normal person in this whole family. He glared at Franny's unmade bed and the piles of clothes surrounding it. *That* certainly isn't normal, he thought. Maybe she's afraid of hurting herself if she falls out of bed.

My mother is too old to be dating, he fumed, sitting on the edge of his bed and putting on his socks. She's my *mother*, for Chrissake! What would she and Mr. Raven do on a date, anyway? Make out? Hold hands? Kiss? Mothers aren't supposed to do things like *that*.

Martin grabbed his jacket and stormed out of the house without eating breakfast. Another beautiful day, Martin thought. And I have to be in school.

As Martin walked to school, a vivid image formed in his mind. His mother and Mr. Raven were tooling down the highway in a red convertible with the top down. Mr. Raven's left hand was draped over the wheel. His right arm was wrapped around Martin's mother, who was snuggled up against Mr. Raven, her eyes closed like a purring cat's. The wind bubbled through her hair.

A silly smile underscored Mr. Raven's beaklike nose. He had a cigarette jammed into a corner of his mouth, sticking up. He looks like ants are crawling up his pant legs, Martin thought, and he's trying not to laugh.

As Martin neared school, the scene in his head changed. He saw his mother emerge from a brightly lit bathroom, dressed in a nightgown so thin that the light shone through it, silhouetting all the curves of her body. The airy fabric swirled as she walked toward Mr. Raven, who was sitting up in a bed, the covers pulled up to his bare chest. Under his nose was the same silly grin as before. The ants are probably in his underwear, Martin thought. And he likes the way they feel.

That's disgusting! Martin thought. He ran, trying to escape the images haunting his head. The late bell rang. The images tumbled out.

"Good morning, Martin," Mr. Raven said, as Martin rushed into the room. Mr. Raven smiled.

Martin flung himself into his seat and tried not

to breathe hard. Son of a bitch, he thought, frowning at Mr. Raven.

"You're just in time."

In time for what? Martin asked himself bitterly. Being in time for school is as thrilling as being on time for the dentist.

"Before we begin," Mr. Raven said, "I have a new seating arrangement for all of you." The class groaned. Mr. Raven was always searching for a seating arrangement that would keep everybody quiet. He's more stupid than a dead snake, Martin thought. You either become friends or enemies of the people you sit next to. Either way, sooner or later, you make noise. Even an idiot would know that by now.

"Clyde, close the door, please, so that we don't disturb the other classes."

Martin watched kids push around desks and tried to figure out what messages Mr. Raven was sending people in the class.

Mr. Raven is tired of Carrie and Bess passing notes across the aisle, Martin observed. Carrie was now in the back of the room, next to Mr. Raven's desk. Bess was now in the front by the door.

Mr. Raven is also tired of Barney and Clyde's antics, Martin thought, smugly. Maybe he knows Clyde was the one who brought that cherry stuff to school. Barney was now in the front row in the middle and Clyde was in the back corner next to Mickey's cage.

"Martin." Mr. Raven looked up from his seating chart. "I'd like you behind Barney, here in the second row."

Of all the stupid things Mr. Raven has ever done, Martin fumed as he pushed his desk toward Barney's, this is the stupidest. Doesn't he know we're enemies? Is he blind? Maybe he's trying to get Barney and me back together. Maybe *that's* what Mom and he talked about last night. Well, they can just forget it.

Barney twisted in his seat as Martin positioned his desk behind Barney's. "Better watch it, Traitor," Barney whispered, under his breath.

Martin's heart sank. "Traitor?"

"Yeah. You tried to make Mr. Raven think I took that stuff from his desk. Creep-o!"

"I did not," Martin whispered back. He sat down.

"Don't lie like a dirty wet dog," Barney whispered through clenched teeth. "Just watch it."

Martin leaned forward. "Watch what?" Martin whispered. "The fat wart on the back of your head?" Martin smiled and sat back. "Where your brain is?"

Barney grunted as he turned toward the front. I don't know why I ever wanted *you* as a friend, Martin thought. He stared at Barney's red Hawaiian shirt. *That shirt's as ugly as you.*

"OK, class," Mr. Raven said, after the desks were rearranged. "Let's start the math quiz." He slid off his stool, walked over to a round table in a front corner of the room, and grabbed a pile of papers. He flicked through the papers. "Take one and pass the rest back." He walked to the next row. "I will not answer questions during this quiz." He licked his thumb and continued flicking. "If you can't do a problem, skip to the next one." He moved to Barney's row. "If you finish early, please turn your paper over and get out a book to read."

Barney handed the papers back, over his shoulder. Martin reached and Barney let them go as Martin's fingers touched them. Papers fluttered to the floor. "Oops," Barney said, turning around in his seat. "How clumsy of me."

Martin collected the papers. He thought back to the worms he plopped into Barney's soup. *They must have gone to his head.*

Mr. Raven finished counting and walked back to his stool and sat down. "No talking . . ." He looked at Carrie. " . . . and keep your eyes on your own paper." He looked at Harold. "Any questions?" Mr. Raven scanned the classroom, his eyebrows raised. "OK."

Martin looked over the quiz. Quiz, fizz, biz. Fractions, ractions, actions. These don't look so hard, Martin thought. He picked up his pencil. I can do these.

Barney fidgeted, shifting his weight from one cheek to the other. Martin looked up. What a shirt! he thought again. There ought to be a rule about shirts like that in school. Jerk! he thought. Before he could stop himself, Martin poked Barney with the sharp point of his pencil, right in the middle of one of the flowers. Barney's head jerked up as if he'd been stung by a bee. Muttering, Barney lurched to his feet. Mr. Raven looked up from his reading. Barney pointed to his pencil and made a cranking motion with his arm. Mr. Raven nodded and resumed reading.

Barney's face was grim as he turned around. He quickly jabbed his pencil at Martin's quiz as he walked past on his way to the pencil sharpener. Anger flushed

Martin's face as he looked down at his paper. A rough pencil line split the paper from top to bottom. The paper was torn along part of the dark line.

*What do I do now?* Martin stared. Thoughts ground in his head like the pencil being sharpened behind him. What will Mr. Raven say?

Too late, Martin heard Barney approaching from behind. Quick as a rattlesnake, Barney lunged with his newly sharpened pencil at Martin's quiz while Martin reached to cover his paper with both hands. He felt a sharp pain.

Martin looked down. Barney's hand let go of the pencil. The pencil wobbled back and forth, upright, stuck into the fleshy web between Martin's right thumb and forefinger.

A bead of blood popped up around the wood and crawled down the ravine in Martin's folded skin. The root of his thumb began to throb.

Mr. Raven looked up impatiently. "Barney, you aren't looking at Martin's quiz, are you?" Barney swallowed and shook his head. He glanced at Mr. Raven and then at the pencil. The bead left a shiny trail on Martin's skin, which greased the way for a trickle of blood.

"Then what *are* you doing?" One by one, kids looked over at Barney and Martin. Mr. Raven slid off his stool and walked toward them.

"I didn't mean to do it." Barney's voice was small, as if he were talking to himself. He watched, frightened, as Mr. Raven approached. "I didn't mean to do it," he said. His voice trembled.

*This hasn't happened.* Martin closed his eyes, but

he saw the pencil sticking up like an arrow without feathers, quivering in his hand. He was afraid to move, afraid that it would hurt more than it already did.

"Now, Barney . . ." Mr. Raven quickened his pace. "Barney, you know that — " Mr. Raven stopped and stared. "What is going on here?"

Martin was pale.

"I didn't mean to do it," Barney said. His lower lip quaked.

Pamela, who sat behind Martin, leaned over Martin's shoulder. "Oh, yuck," she said. "He's bleeding."

"Everybody back to your quizzes," Mr. Raven barked. He walked up to Barney. "Sit down," he ordered.

Barney crumpled into his seat. He folded his arms on his desktop and laid his face in them.

Mr. Raven dropped down on one knee beside Martin's desk. He stared at the pencil in Martin's hand.

*It's all your fault!* Martin fought tears as he looked at Mr. Raven's face. *Son of a bitch.*

"Here, let me take this out," Mr. Raven said quietly. He touched the pencil gingerly and pulled slowly. The wood above the lead was pink. Martin grimaced.

It will hurt less if I pull it quickly, Mr. Raven thought, gripping the pencil tighter and yanking. He felt the tip of sharpened lead snap inside Martin's skin.

Martin winced. He stared at the pencil in Mr. Raven's hand. The lead was broken off halfway up. Why did you put me in back of Barney? Martin screamed inside his head. Why?

The hole in Martin's skin quickly filled with blood. Martin plugged it with the thumb of his other hand. The saltiness of his thumb stung the torn flesh.

"We should get this cleaned up," Mr. Raven said to Martin. He stood up. "I don't want anybody to say *anything* while I'm gone. I'll be back in a minute."

\* \* \*

The school nurse was at another school, so Mr. Raven left Martin with Mr. Clove. Mr. Clove got out the first-aid kit and tried to extract the pencil lead with tweezers. Each time Mr. Clove eased the tweezers in, Martin's hand tensed and jerked away.

Mr. Clove sighed and put the tweezers down. "Tell me what happened," he said, looking at Martin.

Martin sat stony-faced.

"Lead just jump in on its own?" Mr. Clove joked. Martin looked over to the corner of the room, trying to keep from crying.

"Well," Mr. Clove said, after a couple of seconds, "let's clean this up and get you back to class."

Mr. Clove poured hydrogen peroxide onto Martin's hand. They watched it bubble around the wound in silence.

"Will I get lead poisoning?" Martin asked as the bubbles melted into his skin.

"No," Mr. Clove replied. He smiled. "You'll still have unleaded blood." Martin didn't respond and Mr. Clove quit smiling. "Pencil lead isn't really lead at all. It's graphite, carbon — like charcoal. It will probably just work its way out."

Or work its way in, Martin thought.

When Martin got back to the classroom, his desk was no longer behind Barney's. Carrie was in front of Martin, where Barney used to be, and Barney was in the back, right in front of Mr. Raven's desk.

* * *

When he got home, Martin didn't tell his mother or Franny what had happened. He waited to see how long it would take before either of them noticed.

It didn't take long.

"What happened to your hand?" Franny asked, as she helped Martin set the table for dinner.

"Nothing much," Martin said, trying to act unconcerned. The pencil only hurt like a thousand shots of insulin, he bragged to himself.

"Then why is it taped up like that?"

"Well," Martin said, bursting to tell, but trying to be cool, "if you have to know, Barney stabbed me today with his pencil."

Franny looked across the table at Martin. "I heard that somebody was stabbed in school today but I thought they meant a knife and I thought it was a joke," she said, raising her eyebrows. "A pencil? Barney?"

Martin walked into the kitchen for the plates. Franny was right behind him.

"And it wasn't an accident?" Franny asked, reaching around their mother and picking up a bowl of steaming mashed potatoes. "You mean he *meant* to stab you?"

"Franny, would you put a little butter on that before . . ." She turned around, still holding the potroast pan with her oven gloves. "What did you say?"

She looked at Franny and then she looked at Martin. Her gaze stopped at Martin's hand. "What happened to your hand, Martin?" she asked, her eyes sweeping up, connecting with his.

"Oh, nothing," he said. He walked up to the cabinets and opened a cabinet door. He took down three plates. His thumb muscle tensed as he held the plates and the tape pinched into the root of his thumb.

"Martin." Her patience was wearing thin. "What happened to your hand?" She wasn't merely asking a question, she was giving an order.

So, as the three of them carried the food out to the table and sat down, Martin described Barney stabbing him, leaving out the part about poking Barney with his pencil, and making sure that his mother understood that it was Mr. Raven's fault for moving him behind Barney in the first place.

"You and Barney used to be such good friends," Mrs. Enders said as she helped each of them to some meat. "I don't know why you're doing these things to each other. Mr. Raven even told me that he heard something about worms in . . ." She stopped, and looked at Martin, embarrassed. "Yes, last night Mr. Raven and I talked a little bit about you and Barney," she said. "He's puzzled too." She handed Martin his plate.

That's great! Martin thought. Just great! So they *were* talking about me last night!

"And I thought about you today," Mrs. Enders continued. "It was wrong of me not to tell you that I was going out to eat with Mr. Raven. I apologize."

She helped herself to potatoes. "But that doesn't mean I wouldn't have gone out with him anyway. And I want you to know that I invited Mr. Raven to go on a picnic with us this Saturday. To the Ledges."

Martin's stomach sank and his appetite disappeared. *We're going on a picnic with Mr. Raven?* He stared at his mother and slumped back into his chair.

"Martin," she said, "I want you to understand. Mr. Raven is a very nice man."

Yeah, he's so nice he tempted Barney to stab me by moving me next to him, Martin thought.

"And," his mother continued, "I don't want you to think that anything serious is going on between us. He's just somebody I would like to get to know better . . . somebody I think would be nice as a friend."

"I don't know," said Franny.

"I won't go!" Martin exploded. "You talk about me behind my back with my teacher. And then invite him on a picnic without asking first because you know I'd say no!" He glared at the food on his plate. Butter was melting down the pile of mashed potatoes. The meat was steaming — and so was he. "What if the kids at school find out?" Martin yelled, his eyes flashing. "What would they say if they saw me having a picnic with Mr. Raven?"

"That's enough, Martin," his mother said sternly. "He's been invited and you will join us."

Frustration flooded Martin. She doesn't care about me, he thought. All she cares about is Mr. Raven.

Martin ate mechanically. He didn't taste the food. He hardly chewed. What if his dad found out about all of this? he wondered. Would he come back and tell Mr. Raven to bug off? Naw, Martin decided, he'd probably just stay in Alaska with his moose and grizzly bears.

After dinner, Martin trudged to his room, slammed the door shut, and grabbed his spiral-ring notebook. He opened it to the letter he'd written to his dad.

"P.S.," he wrote. "I just thought I'd let you know that somebody tried to kill me today. Not that you would care. Your wife and my mother (remember her?) doesn't care either. In fact, she has the hots for my teacher who tried to get me killed. He put me next to my worst enemy who stabbed me with his pencil. You probably remember him. He's a lot like you. His name is Barney. You always liked him best anyway. Better luck next time."

He signed it: "Your worst enemy, Martin Enders."

Martin lay back in his bed and read over the letter. I hate feeling this way, he thought. But I can't help it. Everybody is so stupid all of a sudden.

# Chapter 9

Martin yanked the sheet of his bed up, folded it back over the blanket, and tucked his side under the mattress. An ant couldn't crawl into this bed now, Martin thought, brushing his hand over the taut sheet.

"Make your bed so that you need a shoehorn to get inside," his father told him each Saturday morning when the family traded dirty sheets for clean ones. If his bed wasn't just right, his father would rip apart the bed Martin had just made, drop the sheets and blankets on the floor, and watch Martin make it again — and again and again if he had to. This was the one practice Mr. Enders carried on from his Marine training — otherwise, he was just as sloppy as Franny.

I learned how to make beds, Martin thought, just the way Dad liked. He frowned. It was about the only thing I learned to do the way he liked. He looked over at Franny, who was trying to smooth her bedspread over sheets and blankets that were as wrinkled as an old lady's face. He watched her toss some stuffed animals over the lumpy parts of the bedspread.

What would she do if I walked up to her bed and ripped it apart, just like Dad used to do to me? he wondered. She'd probably just plop her junk back on the bed and smooth it out again, he thought. Martin grimaced as she slid some books and stuffed animals under her bed with her toes.

"Well, that didn't take very long." Franny faced Martin, a big smile on her face. "I'll go help Mom get the picnic ready."

The picnic. Martin had tried, but he couldn't think of a good excuse for not going on the picnic. When he was Barney's friend, the two of them would disappear on their bikes after breakfast, forget the time accidently on purpose, and come home after everybody was gone. I could always do that by myself, he thought.

"I'm not going," he said. A stuffed dog had trespassed onto his side of the room and Martin kicked it toward Franny. Its floppy ears fluttered like wings as it flew through the air. When Franny was younger, kicking one of her stuffed animals would have caused a nasty fight. Martin watched Franny stoop, not bending her knees, and pick it up. She looked like a scarecrow with poles stuck up its pant legs.

"I think you're being unreasonable, Martin," Franny said, plopping the stuffed dog in the middle of her bed. She sat down on the edge of her bed and bedspread wrinkles drained toward her bottom like water rushing down a sink.

"She can't make me go," Martin said, putting his

hands on his hips. "I'll just run off and not come back until you've left."

Franny frowned. "Martin, Mom would just wait until you came back, even if it took all day. You'd just make everybody miserable."

"Yeah?" Martin spread his feet shoulder-width apart. "Just like she's making me miserable? It would serve her right," he said, staring at Franny defiantly.

"Martin." Franny talked slowly and clearly, as if she were talking to a two-year-old, which made Martin want to act like a two-year-old. "I think we should give Mr. Raven a chance. I think — "

"I don't care what you think," Martin said, turning to face the bedroom window. The sky was bright blue with no clouds. Earlier, when he was climbing out of his deep sleep, he'd listened for rain on the roof, hoping the picnic would have to be called off. But when he opened his eyes, he saw nothing but blue sky.

"This is important to Mom," Franny said, sighing. "I think you're being unreasonable. All you're thinking about is yourself."

If I don't think about myself, nobody else will, Martin thought, clenching his jaw. Mom doesn't think about me. All she thinks about is *herself*.

"Look," Franny said, standing up, "I'll make a deal with you. If you go today I'll take you to a movie and . . . and I'll pay."

Martin turned to look at her, surprised. Franny was a world-class tightwad. She never treated him to anything. *Is she joking?* Martin saw she was serious.

He relaxed his jaw. Well, maybe I'll go this once, he thought. It won't be fun. And Franny will probably want to treat me to some crummy lovey-dovey movie. Maybe if she let me choose. . . .

Franny's face split into a grin. "And you can choose the movie." She turned to the door. "Come on. Let's go help Mom."

Without a word, Martin followed Franny to the kitchen.

Their mother was sticking a pan of chicken into the oven. She closed the oven door and wiped her hands on her apron. "I'm glad you two are here now. I'm running way behind and still need to make potato salad. Would you get the boiled potatoes from the refrigerator, Franny?"

Franny walked over to the refrigerator. She opened the door, pulled out a bowl of potatoes, and lifted them up to the counter with a shrug. "I suppose I should start cutting these up?" She smiled at her mother.

"I suppose so," Mrs. Enders said. "Martin, would you clean up those dishes in the sink?" Martin walked silently to the sink and reached into the soapy water. He grabbed the sponge and scrubbed at a mixing bowl. It was always a mystery to him how clean dishes came out of slimy dishwater that had bits of food and flecks of grease floating around in it.

When Martin finished, he dried his hands on the dish towel. The pads of his fingertips were puckery and gray from the dishwater, and they felt greasy.

He looked at the spot where Barney had stabbed

him. He'd taken off the bandage that morning. His hand had felt naked, but without the pinching tape his thumb had moved smoothly and without pain. The little round scab was soft and gooey and looked like one of the pieces of meat that were left in the sink's strainer when he let out the dishwater.

"Martin, would you chop the onions?" his mother asked, rummaging around in the refrigerator. She pulled out a plastic sack in which two large red onions dangled.

He shook his head as he got out the chopping board. Kneeling on a chair, he peeled off the brittle, papery layers of the onion. Grasping the knife, he carved uneven slabs from the onion.

"What are we having for dessert?" Franny asked.

"Apple pie," Mrs. Enders said.

Apple pie. Martin frowned and blinked as fumes from the onion scorched his eyes. Apple pie was Dad's favorite dessert. Martin scrunched his eyes harder and a tear squeezed out of one corner. It slid down his cheek and landed on the cutting board. Salty tears will make the onions taste better, Martin thought.

Apple pie. Dad ate his apple pie with a bit of cheddar cheese for each bite. Sometimes, when there was some pie left over, he and I would sneak into the kitchen late in the evening and share what was left, Martin thought.

Martin rocked the knife faster, back and forth, mincing the onion slices. Another tear popped from his eye. So what? Martin said to himself. Why should I care about apple pie and Dad and Mr. Raven?

But he wondered if he wasn't chopping onions if he would feel like crying anyway.

* * *

*This must be it.*

Sitting in his car, Mr. Raven looked at the scrap of paper in his hand. "One-o-six Columbus," he said. He looked up at the house again. It was 106 Columbus, all right.

He turned off the engine. "In fourteen ninety-two, Columbus sailed the ocean blue." The rhythm of his rhyme matched the beating of his heart — in fourteen, thump-thump, ninety, thump-thump, two, thump-thump. Mr. Raven pictured the numbers in his head and without thinking stacked fourteen on top of ninety-two and added them up. The answer was 106!

Mr. Raven got out of the car and studied the house. It was like all the other houses in the neighborhood — red brick, one story, boxy. The yard had been hastily mown, with tufts of grass sticking up like punk cowlicks.

He walked up the sidewalk to the front door. As he reached for the doorbell, the door flew open.

"Mr. Raven!" Franny's smiling face popped out. "Come in."

Mr. Raven stepped inside. "Hope I'm not too early," he said.

"Mom is getting everything together in the kitchen," Franny said, striding into the living room. "Why don't you sit down," she said, waving toward the couch, "and I'll go see if Mom needs help."

Franny disappeared and Mr. Raven sat down and looked across the room. On the opposite wall was a modern painting of a matador. Without a bull, the matador looked as if he was merely tangled in his cape and struggling to wrestle free. I sometimes feel like that when I wake up in the morning after strange dreams, he thought.

Suddenly his nose tingled. The feeling spread across his face and he sneezed messily into one of his hands. His hand moved and he felt something tugging at his nose. Oh boy, Mr. Raven thought. He reached into his jacket with his free hand and pulled out a wad of tissue. Mr. Raven wiped off his hand and blew his nose. Where should I put this? he wondered, looking around the living room. Not seeing a wastebasket, he folded the tissue on itself and stuck the whole gloppy mess into his jacket pocket. I'll get rid of this later, he thought.

"Tom." Mrs. Enders was carrying a paper sack in the crook of each arm. "I think we're ready." She was wearing jeans and a red and black checkered flannel shirt.

"Let me help you with those." Mr. Raven stood up.

"Thanks, but I'm all right," Mrs. Enders said. She turned her head. "Martin, are you ready?" she called.

Franny bounded into the room. "He's coming. He's making a pit stop." They heard a toilet flush. A door opened and Martin walked into the living room, wiping the palms of his hands on his jeans.

"Hi, Martin." Mr. Raven tried to make his voice smile as much as his face. Martin stared at him grimly. "I guess we're off . . . like a dirty shirt!"

They walked toward Mr. Raven's car. Mr. Raven
tried to open the trunk and found it was locked. Without thinking, he jammed his hands into his jacket pockets for the car keys. Goo oozed from the wad of tissue
onto his right hand.

He felt the keys in his left pocket. Without taking
his right hand out of its pocket, Mr. Raven unlocked
the trunk and lifted its lid. Franny helped her mother
set the sacks into the trunk while Mr. Raven walked
to Martin, who was standing by the front door on the
passenger side.

"It's locked," Martin said.

"Better tie my shoe," Mr. Raven said, handing
the keys to Martin. He dropped to one knee and pretended to fumble around with his laces, wiping the
goo off his right hand onto the top of his sock.

"Let's go." Mr. Raven smiled sheepishly, stood
up, and took the keys from Martin.

*   *   *

What a pit, Martin thought, looking at his feet.
The floor of the car was littered with candy-bar wrap-
pers and papers and a single dirty sock. And this heap
rattles like it's dragging a bumper. Martin looked at
the countryside streaming by. His elbow was braced
against the window and his chin was cupped in the
palm of his hand. His fingers, curled under his nose,
smelled like the onions he'd cut up. Franny's elbows
were hooked over the front seat, between Mr. Raven
and her mother. Martin tuned out their chattering.

That morning as he dressed, Martin had reached
for his father's faded blue work shirt with the oil stain
on the left shoulder. His father had forgotten it and

Martin had rescued it from a pile of dirty laundry and hung it, unwashed, in his closet. It smelled like his father — deodorant mixed with sweat and body odor, especially in the armpits, and the vague smells of oil and sawdust. Martin had surprised himself by wanting to wear it. And as they drove along, he enjoyed the way it smelled.

They pulled into the gravel road that led to the Ledges. The bumps jarred his head and jammed his elbow into the window. Martin sat up and folded his hands in his lap. They pulled into the parking lot of a picnic area.

"I'm surprised we're the only ones here," Mr. Raven said, getting out.

Martin was relieved.

They gathered the picnic things together and walked toward a group of picnic tables surrounded by trees.

"This is a wonderful spot," Mrs. Enders said, walking up to a table set off from the others.

Yeah, Martin thought. Only three dog turds within sight and only a dozen splotches of bird doo on the table's top.

"Finally," Mr. Raven said, putting a bag on the end of the table. "And," he said, setting another bag on the ground, "I brought some balls and a Frisbee in case anybody wants to play catch."

"I haven't thrown a softball in ages." Mrs. Enders smiled. "That sounds like fun."

Fun, fun, fun, Martin thought. Almost as much fun as folding laundry.

Mr. Raven reached into the sack and brought out

a grass-stained softball. "Looks like a good place to spread out over there," he said, pointing to a field of grass.

They walked to the grass and formed a lopsided square — Mrs. Enders threw to Franny, Franny threw to Mr. Raven, Mr. Raven threw to Martin, and Martin threw back to his mother. The longest side of the square was between Mr. Raven and Martin.

Martin watched Mr. Raven while everybody chattered. Mr. Raven's form was fluid and loose. Not as wimpy as I expected, Martin thought, but pretty wimpy compared to Dad's.

"Not so hard, Martin," his mother called, chasing the ball.

"Let's try some grounders," Mr. Raven shouted to Martin. He caught Franny's toss, threw up his right leg, pivoted on his left, and threw an underhand worm-burner. Martin crouched, ready for the ball to slip right into his cupped hands. Instead, the ball hit a stick, bounced, and dribbled through his legs.

"Nice try," Mr. Raven shouted as Martin ran after it. Mr. Raven's voice was fat with encouragement.

"Why the hell did you do that?" Martin muttered. He picked up the ball, pivoted like a pro, and threw his arm back so far that he almost touched his butt. He heaved the ball with a grunt toward Mr. Raven instead of to his mother.

Martin thought he heard the ball hum as it zoomed toward Mr. Raven. Mr. Raven was turned toward Franny, who was laughing at whatever he was saying. Martin watched as the ball zeroed in on Mr. Raven's head, growing smaller and smaller. If it grows any smaller, Martin thought, fascinated, it will turn into a bullet.

"Watch out!" Mrs. Enders yelled.

Startled, Mr. Raven turned toward her and the ball bonked him squarely at the top of his forehead, smacking like a bat connecting for a homer. His head snapped back. "Uh!" Mr. Raven grunted and crumpled to the ground.

"Tom, are you all right?" Mrs. Enders ran toward him.

Franny beat her mother, sliding into Mr. Raven feet first, as if she were stealing a base. Mr. Raven struggled to sit up and Franny helped his head into her lap. "Mom, do we have some ice?" she asked.

"Yes. In one of the bags." She looked up to where Martin was standing, rooted to the ground. "Martin, bring us some ice and a napkin. Now!"

*It was an accident. It was an accident.* Martin trotted mechanically to the food. He didn't know whom to feel sorry for, himself or Mr. Raven. If Mr. Raven hadn't been gabbing with Franny, Martin thought angrily, it wouldn't have happened.

As Martin rummaged through the sacks, he was surprised to see a bottle of wine. Jesus Christ, he thought. Mom hasn't bought wine or beer since Dad left. Martin grabbed the corkscrew and thrust it into the pocket of his jacket.

Martin punched a hole in the bag of ice, took several cubes and a napkin, and walked back. He handed his mother the ice wrapped in the napkin. His mother took it without a word and pressed it against Mr. Raven's forehead.

"I'm OK." Mr. Raven squinted at Martin. He gently pushed Mrs. Enders's hand to one side and explored the red lump growing where his scalp and forehead met. "Look, a bump. More room for my brain," he said.

Martin wanted to say he was sorry and didn't want to say he was sorry. He was angry with himself and he was angry at Mr. Raven for getting hurt. Why do these things happen to me, anyway? Martin fumed.

Mr. Raven looked up at him. "That's OK, Martin. It was an accident," he said. He started to smile, but his mouth jumped as Mrs. Enders moved the ice to the other side of the lump. "No need for apologies."

Was that a hint or what? Martin wondered angrily. Franny frowned at him. She shifted weight off the leg that was falling asleep, trying at the same time to hold Mr. Raven's head still.

"I'm sorry," Martin mumbled.

"I bet," Franny said.

"*I'm sorry*," Martin said loudly. "It was an accident."

"That's OK." Mr. Raven sat up and reached for Martin's hand. He almost pulled Martin down trying to stand up. "But maybe that's enough catch for now."

They walked to the shade of the picnic table. Martin walked behind everybody else.

"These things happen," Martin heard Mr. Raven say to Franny.

"I think you should rest for a while," Mrs. Enders said.

"*I* think we should go for a walk," Mr. Raven said.

"The forest is loaded with wildflowers at this time of year."

"Are you sure you're OK?" Mrs. Enders hesitated.

"I think a walk would do us all some good." Although the bump was bright red, Mr. Raven looked better. "Get us hungry for lunch."

Martin watched the others veer toward the trailhead. His mother stopped and turned. "Come on, Martin. You can help us identify the flowers."

Martin wanted to go and didn't want to go. The nature trail had been one of his father's favorite places. He often brought Barney and Martin to walk it, especially in the spring and the fall, to look at the flowers or to wade through the red, yellow, and brown leaves.

"Come on," Franny called over her shoulder. She was holding Mr. Raven's hand. "Maybe we'll see some deer."

Martin jammed his hands into the pockets of his jeans and scuffed the ground with the tip of his right sneaker. He rubbed his nose against the shoulder of his shirt. The smell of the shirt and the thought of walking the nature trail made him miss his dad. And that made Martin angry. Why should I miss him? Martin thought. He doesn't miss me.

If they ask one more time, Martin thought, I'll go.

"Mar-tin." Franny's voice sounded like a grackle's. "Come on!"

The dark forest floor was spotted with sunlight. The breeze smelled of mushrooms and rotting wood and moldering leaves. Martin recognized a Solomon's seal along the path, its tiny greenish-white flowers hanging like dainty earrings from its stalk.

The other three walked ahead of him. He couldn't see them but he heard laughter and voices filter through the underbrush, softened by a breeze. The oaks and maples and elms arched their gnarled arms over his head. As the wind ruffled their leaves, Martin imagined the trees dancing, swaying stiffly, like old people.

Critters scurried through the forest floor. He watched for a patch of poison ivy that he and Barney used to joke about using for toilet paper.

Martin remembered one time he'd gone to the bathroom just beyond the poison ivy, in some sumac bushes. He'd grabbed some nearby leaves to wipe with. The leaves had crumbled and pieces had stuck to Martin's bottom, making him itch. The itching grew stronger during their walk. Martin had been afraid that he'd mistakenly used dried-up poison ivy leaves.

The trail ended close to where it began. As Martin walked into the sunlight he saw his mother, sister, and Mr. Raven taking food out of the sacks and arranging it on the picnic table. His mother and sister were laughing and Mr. Raven was talking.

Martin hadn't seen his mother this happy for a long time. If she'd only tried a little harder to be happy, Martin thought as he walked toward them, maybe she and Dad would still be together.

"That is a beautiful hike," Mr. Raven said. "Don't you think, Martin?"

"No, he doesn't think," Franny piped up, smiling, "unless he has to."

"Franny." Their mother gave Franny a warning

glance. She turned to Martin. "I remember how you used to come here with your father and Barney. You'd get so excited. . . ."

Martin silently straddled the picnic table's bench and sat.

"Oh, look," his mother said, pulling the bottle of wine out of her sack. "A little surprise!"

Martin felt the corkscrew in his pocket and watched his mother hunt for it. "I could have sworn I put the corkscrew in the sack," she said, exasperated.

"That's all right," Mr. Raven said. "I'd fall asleep if I had wine at this time of day."

Martin smiled and watched them dig into the food.

"This is great potato salad," Mr. Raven said with his mouth full.

"Save some room for dessert," Franny said. "We brought apple pie."

"Oh, boy," Mr. Raven said, scooping up more potato salad. "My favorite."

Martin turned his back on the food, and looked toward the woods. He set his plate on his knees. He was sick of listening to them and watching them chew their chicken bones like dogs.

And Mr. Raven and his mother were having too good a time. Even without the corkscrew.

Martin took a bite of chicken and wiped the grease off his mouth onto the sleeve of his father's shirt. Martin smiled. The more I wear his shirt, the more it will smell like me.

# Chapter 10

Click.

Franny groped toward her bed. "Good night, Martin," she said, pulling back the covers and crawling under. She sighed, turned on her side, and hugged her pillow.

Martin stared out the window. The clouds floated by the moon so fast that Martin imagined the house moving, flying past the moon and into space.

Martin sighed and looked toward Franny. After looking at the moon, his eyes were unaccustomed to the room's dark. But, as in an instant photograph, a lump slowly developed in the middle of Franny's bed. He could see the hill of her hip and her dark hair against the white sheets. Guess I better get it over with, he thought.

"Franny," he began, "I'd like to make a deal with you."

"Not now, Martin," Franny said, rolling onto her other side and facing her wall. "I'm tired."

"Come on, Franny," Martin said, raising himself on his elbow. "All you have to say is 'Yes.' "

"Mar-tin," Franny said. "Good night."

"And if you say yes, I'll let you practice giving shots on me," Martin said.

Franny flipped onto her back and sat up. "You'll what?"

Franny's eye sockets were dark shadows in the silvery moonlight. "You heard me," he said drily. "But if you don't care" — he lay down and turned his back toward her — "that's OK. Good night."

"Wait just a minute," Franny said, sitting on her legs and crossing her arms. "I'd love to practice on you. Tell me what you want."

"And you'll do it?" Martin grinned to himself.

"Of course not," Franny said. "But I'll consider doing it."

"Well, OK." Martin turned over and propped his head on his elbow and hand. "Mom's been seeing an awful lot of Mr. Raven lately and I think we should find out more about him." He'd rehearsed this speech a dozen times in his head and he didn't want to leave anything out. He took a deep breath. "I think we should see where he lives, see if he's into things we don't know about — drugs or parties or something."

"Martin, that's crazy. Do you want to break into his apartment or something?"

Martin tried not to smile. "I guess we could do that," he said. "That's one way to find out more about him."

"That's illegal, Martin. Besides, Mr. Raven is a very nice man. He makes Mom happy."

"We wouldn't take anything or do anything wrong. Besides, that's not the point." Martin's voice rose. More quietly, he continued, "We know he was divorced, but we don't know why. Maybe he beat his wife or went out with other women. Maybe he drank too much or spent money on drugs."

"That's silly, Martin, and you know it." Franny reached behind, retrieved her pillow, and hugged it. "Besides, we could just talk to his ex-wife if we wanted to find out. We wouldn't have to break into his apartment."

"Do you know her name or where she lives?" Martin asked.

"No."

"Do you want to ask Mr. Raven how we can get ahold of her?"

"Of course not." Martin could feel Franny's glare.

"Well, the only place we might find out is his apartment. Maybe he has an old letter or something lying around that will give us a clue." Martin fought the excitement in his voice. "Look, we don't even know if we'll be able to get inside or find anything. But we gotta try."

"Well, I don't like it."

"I don't either," Martin lied. "But we've gotta do something."

"Sure. And what if we get caught?" Franny lay down on her back and pulled the covers up to her chin.

"We won't," Martin said. "Look. I'll even forget about the movie you owe me." He nibbled his lower lip nervously and held his breath.

Franny closed her eyes. "Good night," she said.

Martin tried not to plead. "Remember, you can practice on me."

Franny turned her back to him. "I *said*, 'Good night.' "

Martin eased under his covers. I hope she'll do it, he thought. She didn't say no. Martin had heard stories about bachelors — how they never washed their dishes and how they read dirty magazines and how they never picked up. He wanted Franny to see how Mr. Raven lived. Maybe then she would help him talk their mother out of seeing Mr. Raven anymore.

Mr. Raven has been hanging around too much, Martin thought, and I don't like it. And the thing that bothered him the most was how Mr. Raven sometimes sat in his father's chair at the dinner table and the way Franny acted around him. She laughed and joked the same way she used to laugh and joke with their father.

I have to prove to Franny that Mr. Raven isn't such a neat guy. I have to prove that he'd make a lousy father. Mom and Dad aren't even divorced yet, Martin thought. Maybe Dad will come back when he finds out that it's no fun to kill grizzly bears all day long if you can't come home to your wife and kids.

\* \* \*

The next evening, at dinner, Mrs. Enders told Martin and Franny that she and Mr. Raven had a date planned for Friday.

"I'll make macaroni and cheese for your dinner and," she said, smiling, "I'll get some fancy ice cream for your dessert. And," she added, looking from Martin's face to Franny's face, "I'll let you watch TV as late as you want."

What a bribe, Martin thought. But he didn't say anything. His mother's announcement was just the thing Martin had been waiting for.

On Friday evening, before the thud of the front door was swallowed up by silence, Martin and Franny were in their bedroom, peeling off their school clothes. They had had whispered discussions in their darkened bedroom the past two nights to decide what to wear, modeling each suggestion to see how it looked in the dark. Their pale skin glowed fluorescent in the moonlight as they decided to wear dark T-shirts, dark jackets, dark pants, and dark sneakers with dark socks.

Martin grabbed the knapsack that he had stocked for spying: a flashlight, a screwdriver, and a pad of paper and pencil for taking notes.

"Ready?" Martin asked.

"Ready," Franny replied nervously. Her smile was painfully stretched and her nostrils were pinched.

Martin had drawn a map, tracing it from the telephone book. They took an indirect route, walking along side streets. They turned the last corner and saw the apartment complex where Mr. Raven lived, hovering over the houses gathered around it. He was sure Mr. Raven lived on the ground floor of the building closest to them. Barney had gone trick-or-treating at Mr. Raven's on Halloween and told Martin that, besides giving out apples, Mr. Raven lived where they could easily soap his windows.

As they walked up to the apartment building, dusk fell rapidly, covering everything in darkness. They hid behind a large bush near the driveway that led to the building's parking lot until darkness was complete.

"What we should do," Martin explained, "is check out every apartment on the ground floor until we find one that looks like Mr. Raven's."

"What should we look for?" Franny asked.

"I don't know. Beer bottles, maybe, or dirty dishes on the floor."

Franny nodded tensely.

Stars popped out. Bright light from windows fell in long stripes that stretched across the lawns surrounding the building.

"We'll have to stay low," Martin whispered to Franny. "Otherwise people will see us from the road."

"Gotcha," Franny said in her normal voice.

"Sh!" Martin hissed.

"Martin," Franny said, "when people hear whispering they automatically think of people sneaking around. If we talk in a normal tone of voice, people won't even notice us."

"That's not true," Martin whispered. "Spies don't talk out loud. Get the flashlight out of the pack."

"OK," said Franny. They crept up to the corner apartment and positioned themselves below an open window. Just as they were about to stick their heads above the sill a light flicked on inside.

Martin and Franny dropped to the ground. Through the window they heard a woman's voice calling to somebody in another room. "Hon, why don't you pop us a coupla beers and heat up the oven. We have some frozen dinners in the freezer."

Franny sniggered and clapped both of her hands to her mouth, trying to hold it in. The laughter squeezed out of her eyes as tears. Impatiently, Martin motioned for them to move down to the next apartment.

As they crawled along the wall they heard the woman's voice fade as she walked out of the room. "Well, poopsie, we have the whole evening to ourselves. . . ."

*Poopsie*, Martin thought. That sounds like a name for disposable diapers.

Lights were on in the next apartment. Martin and Franny heard the TV and quietly crawled under a window and in front of a sliding glass door with the curtain pulled. They smelled something Italian cooking.

The next apartment was dark. Martin pulled himself up by the windowsill. The curtains were open and Martin peeked inside. He turned on the flashlight and swept the beam from one end of the bedroom to the other. It was a mess. This might be it, he thought.

Martin dropped to his hands and knees and crawled to the sliding glass door. The curtain was partway open. He flashed the light inside. He saw piles of books and magazines propped against the closet wall. Against the door, looking as though they were waiting to be let outside, were the shoes Mr. Raven always wore to school. Holding his breath, Martin reached up and pulled at the door's handle. Open, open, open, he thought to himself. The door slid over. Martin sighed. He hadn't expected to be this lucky. If the door hadn't opened he would have tried using the screwdriver. And then Franny would have objected.

"I don't know about this . . . " Franny said. But before she could finish, Martin had opened the door farther and crawled inside.

"Mar-tin!" Franny said.

"Come on in," Martin said, standing up. "Remember our deal." His skin prickled as he heard steps walking across the ceiling. "Come on!" he whispered.

"Oh, OK," Franny said. She stood and closed the door behind her. "We better not stay very long."

Martin closed the curtain and walked toward a place in the wall where he thought a switch should be. He found a bank of switches and flicked one on. The room filled with light.

Martin and Franny stood facing each other, blinking. He couldn't believe that everything had gone so well.

Martin scanned the room. Books and magazines and newspapers were piled everywhere. Along one wall stretched a set of shelves stacked with more books, a stereo system, and records. Across the room, under a hanging light fixture, was a round table covered with papers and books. As Martin walked closer, he noticed that one stack of papers was the math test on fractions

they'd taken that day. Another stack was the reports
Mr. Raven had assigned for the week — this time on
favorite books.

"Look," Franny said, walking up to the table,
"some letters. Maybe one is from his ex-wife." She
pulled a chair out from the table, sat, and began leafing
through the pile of letters. "Ugh," she said. "Most of
these are bills. Visa . . . Mastercard . . . Sears . . . Oh,
look at this one," she said, picking one up and holding
it toward Martin. "Three hundred and seventy-four
dollars to Amoco. Wow, I didn't know teachers made
enough money for credit cards."

Martin watched Franny take a letter from an envelope. "Who's that from?" he asked.

"His mother," Franny said, scrunching her eyebrows together and reading. "Boy, is her handwriting
bad. And she misspelled 'lovely.' "

Martin leafed through a couple of math tests, looking for his. He'd felt good about the test after he'd
taken it. He hoped that he got all of them right. He
stopped at Barney's. As quickly and quietly as he could,
he folded up Barney's test into fours and stuck it in
his back pocket.

"Nothing in this pile," Franny said, folding the
letter and putting it back in its envelope. "He sure
has a neat mother. She just got back from visiting her
sister in Santa Fe, New Mexico. They got to see Indians and. . ."

"Franny, if you're finished here, maybe you should
go someplace else and look." Martin didn't want to

hear about Indians and Santa Fe, New Mexico. And he didn't want Franny to think Mr. Raven was neat because his mother was neat.

"What are you doing?" Franny asked, walking around to his end of the table.

"Just looking to see if he's graded my report yet," Martin said, leafing through the stack. "I'll be with you in a minute."

"OK," Franny said, walking away. "Just don't change your grade." She smiled and Martin returned her smile halfheartedly.

Martin saw his report close to the top. Like the math tests, it hadn't been graded either. He kept going through the pile. Carrie . . . Bob . . . Sydney . . . Barney. Martin snatched the report from the pile and, reaching behind himself, stuffed it into the unzipped knapsack. Gotcha! he thought, smiling.

"Oh, look, Martin!" Franny called. "A kitchen!"

"Franny, be *quiet!*" Martin whispered as he walked toward Franny's voice. How disappointing, Martin thought as he walked into the small, narrow kitchen. He looked around. Everything was clean. Freshly washed dishes were piled high and draining in a wire basket beside the sink. Martin opened the refrigerator and right in the front of the second shelf were several cans of beer. It wasn't the kind his father liked. It was light beer, the kind his father said was women's beer.

"Want a beer?" he asked Franny, turning around and looking at her.

"Mar-tin, of course not," she said.

"This is sissy beer," Martin said, taking a can out

of the refrigerator. "But since it's the only kind . . ."

Franny snatched it from his hand and glared at him. "Martin, remember we are not going to take anything. Now put this back." She handed Martin the beer.

"I was only joking," Martin said, setting the beer on the top shelf.

"Martin, let's get done and get out of here," Franny said.

"OK," Martin said. "Let's search his bedroom."

They walked down the short hallway that opened onto the bathroom on the right and the bedroom on the left. Martin flicked on the bedroom light.

A sweaty yet sweet smell flavored the air, reminding Martin of locker rooms and perfumy boxes of tissues. Bedcovers and sheets swirled like a storm around the foot of the bed. Two pillows were on the floor. Clothes were piled everywhere. In the corner near the door was a pile of underwear.

"Ooo," Franny said, looking away. "This place is a pit!"

"Yeah." Martin was pleased. This should tell her something about Mr. Raven, he thought. He scanned the room again and his eye stopped on a closet door.

"Why don't you check out that closet, Franny? I'll check his nightstands."

Franny walked toward the closet, but had to stop to clear a path. She picked up a pile of clothes, and started stuffing them in an open dresser drawer.

"Hey," Martin said. "We don't want him to think anybody was here."

Martin walked up to her, took the T-shirts and socks from her hands, and plopped them on the floor. "*You* check the nightstands and *I'll* check the closet," he said.

Franny shrugged and walked toward the bed. "He really is a slob," she said. Takes one to know one, Martin thought, opening the closet door and peering inside. Shoes were piled everywhere and shirts were stuffed along the back, some of them barely clinging to their hangers.

Nothing here, he thought, turning around. Franny was looking through a pile of papers and magazines on a nightstand. "Any dirty magazines?" he asked hopefully.

"No," Franny said, "but he's got some great catalogues."

Great, Martin thought. "I got to take a leak," he said, walking out the bedroom door.

Martin flicked on the bathroom light and closed the door. As he stood in front of the toilet, he looked around. Everything is clean, he noticed. The towels are neatly hung on the towel bar. He looked at the yellowing water. Even the toilet is clean, he thought. I don't see rust stains or yellow splash spots on the rim of the toilet bowl. This bathroom is cleaner than the one at our house. I don't want Franny to see this, he thought.

Martin zipped up and ran his hands under some water. He looked in the mirror. So this is the mirror Mr. Raven looks in when he gets up in the morning. Martin made a face in the mirror. This is what he looks

at when he brushes his teeth or shaves. Or puts on
deodorant, Martin thought, spying a stick deodorant
standing on the countertop.

Martin screwed the cap off the deodorant. The
stick was rounded with hair scratches and a few dark
hairs were imbedded in it. Martin pushed the stick
up and lifted the deodorant to the mirror like a big
piece of chalk.

I shouldn't do this, he thought, his heart beating
faster. This is dumb. But, almost as if his arm were
moving on its own, Martin wrote, in big block letters:
YOU STINK. Martin stared. The pungent odor of deodorant filled the bathroom.

"Martin! What's taking you so long?" Franny's
voice was right outside the door.

"I'm coming, I'm coming," Martin said. "Just a
sec."

That was really dumb, he thought. He grabbed a
towel and rubbed the letters on the mirror. The deodorant smeared but didn't come off. I've really done
it now, Martin thought grimly. Stuffing the towel onto
the rack, Martin flicked off the light, opened the door,
and stepped out into the hall, bumping right into
Franny.

"What were you doing in there?" Franny asked,
trying to look around Martin into the bathroom.

"Nothing," Martin said brusquely, herding her
down the hall. "Did you find anything?"

"No," Franny said. "But I'm glad we came. This
is a neat place. He has some neat stuff. Maybe I can
ask him if I can borrow some of his Hemingway books."

"Yeah," Martin said, sarcastically, "and then he'll wonder how you knew he had Hemingway books."

"I wouldn't ask just like that," Franny said. "Give me a little credit."

My idea backfired, Martin thought. He does have some neat stuff here. And now she likes him even better than before. "Let's get home," he said. "I'm hungry."

But Martin wasn't hungry. And the smell of deodorant lingered in his nose.

Click. He turned off the light and closed the sliding glass door behind them with a thud.

# Chapter 11

—+  +—

Mr. Raven closed his eyes and listened to the sound of pencils softly scritching. That same sound, like fingernails on a window, scratched last night inside his head. He was too sleepy to fight the nightmare images and too awake to ignore them. He imagined dark, hunched shadows lurking outside his window, reaching out like gnarled tree limbs to claw at his screen. And he imagined the gentle brush of doors opening over carpeting or the grind of his sliding glass door moving in its gritty channel like a train derailing.

The moment he walked into his apartment last night, he knew something was wrong. Everything looked the same — the piles of newspapers and the books on the shelves, leaning against each other like tipsy men in a soup line. But he smelled something different, a lingering scent as when someone walks by wearing too much perfume or after-shave.

Mr. Raven crept around the living room, ears as prickly as TV reception in a thunderstorm. His eyes strained to search dark corners. Once he turned his head suddenly and thought he saw the couch jump. The hair on the back of his neck stuck out like porcupine quills, sensitive to slight movements in the hushed air.

This is silly, Mr. Raven thought, realizing that he was stooped in readiness, holding his arms and hands karate-style. But, as silly as he felt, Mr. Raven cautiously peered into the kitchen anyway. The dishes were piled next to the sink, just the way he'd left them. His muscles relaxed.

"Ah ha!" he joked uneasily. He turned to the refrigerator. "Trying to cool your heels in *there!*"

He pulled open the refrigerator door and its glow washed over him. "Thought you could hide behind the orange juice, eh?" Mr. Raven peered inside. His jaw dropped and he stared, open-mouthed, at a can of beer on the top shelf. Mr. Raven glanced down. The rest of the beer was on the second shelf, where he always put it.

Somebody *had* been in his refrigerator! Mr. Raven's heart beat a warning in his ears. *And they might still be in the apartment.* Quietly, he eased the door closed, squeezing the light back into the refrigerator.

As he stalked down the short hall to his bedroom, the smell that greeted him at the door grew stronger. Standing away from the bedroom door, straining to listen, Mr. Raven reached his hand around the door frame, groped for the familiar squareness, and, with a click like a gun cocking, he flipped the switch. His hand shot back as if it were attached to his shoulder by a thick rubber band. He held his breath, listening. Nothing. He jumped into the doorway, crouching, ready to protect himself. His sigh turned into a whimper as he forced the last bit of air from his lungs.

The bedroom looked ransacked — the bed was a rumpled mess, clothes were strewn and piled in corners like fall leaves caught in alleyway eddies. Mr. Raven's forehead relaxed. Everything looked just the way he'd left it.

Mr. Raven's nose tingled and he sniffed. That smell. It was like . . . like his deodorant. Mr. Raven turned, stepped across the hall, and snapped on the light to the bathroom. He gasped.

The dull glow of the mirror made Mr. Raven feel that he was looking through foggy goggles. He took a deep breath, as if he were about to swim underwater. His eyes darted around the bathroom like frightened guppies. They stopped on the toilet. The seat was up. And bright yellow water sat like a puddle of stale beer, a patch of bubbles clinging to the porcelain at the back of the bowl.

Mr. Raven's fear suddenly turned to anger. Before he could stop himself he lashed out, flushing the toilet with his balled-up hand. His fist stung where he hit the lever.

Who could have done this? a voice yelled inside his head. Who could have broken in here and done these things? Who?

And why?

The mirror reflected his shape but no details, like a frosted window melting in the light of a winter morning. Reaching behind him, he grabbed a towel. He brought the towel to his nose and sniffed. Deodorant. He shifted his grip on the towel and felt the stickiness of deodorant cling to his skin.

He dropped the towel and reached for another. Furiously, he rubbed the waxy mirror, leaning over the sink and using both arms. This really stinks, he thought grimly. This really stinks.

Mirroring his anger, his image became blearier the more he rubbed. I need some window cleaner, he thought, throwing the towel onto the counter beside the sink. The stick of deodorant clattered to the floor between the vanity and the toilet.

Mr. Raven stomped to the kitchen. He threw open the refrigerator door and grabbed the beer on the top shelf. Damn it, he thought. I've ruined the fingerprints. And then it struck him. *How did the person break in?*

Mr. Raven threw the unopened beer back into the refrigerator and scurried to his bedroom. He checked the windows. The screens weren't slashed and the windows were locked. Next, he checked the sliding glass door. It was closed, but the latch was up. The door had been unlocked. Mr. Raven snapped the lock down, careful not to touch the rest of the handle. He wanted to preserve fingerprints in case something was missing and he called the police.

That's a laugh, he thought as he walked to the bathroom, a beer in one hand and the window cleaner in the other. "And what evidence do you have that somebody broke in?" he could hear a cop ask. "An unflushed toilet and a misplaced beer and a dirty bathroom mirror? Mr. Raven, that sounds like my house."

His thoughts cleared as his reflection sharpened. This must have been a prank, he thought. Somebody who found the door unlocked and couldn't resist walking in. After all, they didn't *take* the beer, he thought. And they could have wrecked the place — broken things or written on the walls.

But after cleaning the mirror, Mr. Raven cleaned his entire apartment, just to be sure nothing was missing. It took three hours and five beers. Having his apartment broken into made Mr. Raven feel unclean and somehow violated, as if somebody had looked at him and seen him naked underneath his clothes.

Why *did* the person come in? he kept asking himself. Why, why, why? The more he cleaned, the more frustrated Mr. Raven became with that question. He almost wished that something had been taken so that he would know why this had happened. Finally, exhausted, he fell asleep in his clothes. And his dreams were restless and threatening.

Mr. Raven sighed. Maybe I should have called the police anyway, he thought. He woke up with a dull hangover, his head feeling as if it were stuffed with a wet bath towel.

* * *

He heard paper rustling and opened his eyes to survey the class. Heads were still bent over quizzes. Mr. Raven's gaze rested on the back of Martin's head.

The evening with Martin's mother had been wonderful. At first, Mr. Raven avoided talking about school.

But since the picnic, Mr. Raven had been thinking a lot about Martin and about Barney. Eventually, as the evening wore on, he couldn't help himself. He asked Mrs. Enders what she thought of his plan for getting Martin and Barney back together.

Martin was having a hard time expressing his feelings, Mr. Raven explained. He thought that Martin and Barney were still good friends deep down inside. Why else were they so preoccupied with each other? *Something* was bugging each of them about the other, which caused them to express their friendship in very strange ways. Whether they knew it or not, Mr. Raven told Mrs. Enders, Martin and Barney were letting worms and sharpened pencils talk for them. They were trying to express deeply felt emotions, and getting more frustrated all the time.

He understood how Martin felt, Mr. Raven explained. He could remember doing sneaky things when he was a kid instead of saying what he felt. Like the time he'd thrown his brother's alarm clock out of their bedroom window instead of telling him that the ticking kept him awake at night.

One reason he'd never told his brother anything was because his brother never paid any attention when he did. Another reason was that, when he was a kid, Mr. Raven thought that people should just *know* what he was feeling. To tell somebody was like begging a person to understand. Then and now, Mr. Raven didn't like begging.

"Martin and Barney need help telling each other

what they're feeling, what's really bugging them," Mr. Raven concluded.

"I think you're right," Mrs. Enders said. "I think it's worth a try."

So today, even though he didn't feel especially alert or patient, Mr. Raven decided to put his plan into action.

More paper rustled. Several kids, including Barney, were finished with the quiz. Barney sat slumped at his desk, his arms folded over his chest, scowling at the blackboard.

Quickly, before too many kids finished, Mr. Raven scribbled a message on two note cards. He walked around the classroom, checking everybody's progress, keeping order during that awkwardness when some kids are finished and others aren't. He put one card on Martin's desk as he passed by. He left the other on Barney's desk.

The message on both cards was the same. "Please meet me today in the classroom for a business lunch. Thanks. Mr. Raven."

* * *

He knows, Martin thought, feeling his heart sink in his chest. He knows about last night. How could he know? *Anybody* could have done it, Martin thought nervously. For the rest of the morning, Martin couldn't concentrate on anything.

When lunch came, Martin walked slowly back to his classroom with his tray of beans and cut-up hot dogs. Just act natural, he said to himself over and over.

Don't let him think anything's wrong. But Martin's stomach felt like a sack full of wrestling kittens. If I eat anything, he thought, I'll throw up.

Martin stood outside the door for a moment, breathing slowly. He plunged into the classroom.

He almost dropped his tray. Barney was sitting by Mr. Raven, taking food out of his lunch box and arranging it on the table.

"Hello, Martin," Mr. Raven said, looking up and smiling. "Come join us. We were just about ready to start." Barney looked up, surprised.

Anger quieted Martin's nervous stomach. This is just great, he thought, walking grimly to the table. He sat down, away from both of them. Without saying anything, he stabbed a piece of hot dog, popped it into his mouth, and ground his teeth together.

"It's been awhile since we had a business lunch," Mr. Raven began, unwrapping his sandwich.

Barney looked up, smiled weakly, and continued chewing, not knowing what to say. Each time he opened his jaws, his smile became a frown.

"Well," Mr. Raven said, taking a deep breath. His headache, which had disappeared after math, was returning. He didn't know if his plan would work. "I wanted to ask for your advice about something." He tried to keep nervousness from rusting his voice. "I have a problem I can't seem to solve on my own." He picked up his sandwich and took a bite, looking at Barney and then at Martin.

Martin glared at Barney, whose eyebrows were

raised. Barney's really getting into this, Martin thought. Maybe he was spying on me and Franny last night. Maybe *he* told Mr. Raven.

"Yeah?" Barney asked, swallowing. "What's your problem?"

Mr. Raven put down his sandwich. "Let me describe it and then you can tell me what you think."

We didn't do anything, Martin said to himself over and over. We didn't do anything.

Mr. Raven cleared his throat. "I know two people that I met about the same time who were really good friends. They had a lot of fun together and I was just getting to know them when all of a sudden they stopped speaking to each other and started doing nasty things to each other."

Mr. Raven looked at Martin and then at Barney. "This is my problem: I feel caught in the middle. I like them both but I don't know if I'll make one mad by being nice to the other one."

Martin looked at Mr. Raven and then at Barney. Barney was looking at him. He looked back at Mr. Raven. Martin didn't know whether to be relieved or angry. Maybe he doesn't know after all, Martin thought. But what is he trying to do?

"Huh," Martin grunted, stabbing another hunk of hot dog and jamming it into his mouth. He's trying to get us to make up, that's what. Well, Martin thought as he chewed, he's crazy if he thinks we're going to.

"You're talking about us, aren't you?" Barney asked.

"Yes," Mr. Raven admitted.

Before he could stop himself, Martin blurted, "You've been talking to my mother about us, haven't you?" A fleck of food shot across the table.

"Yes," Mr. Raven admitted again.

"Why don't you just leave us alone!" Martin said. "Why don't you just butt out of our lives!"

Mr. Raven studied Martin. "Your mother and I have talked about you because she's concerned about you, Martin." Mr. Raven looked at Barney. His face was frozen in surprise. Mr. Raven looked back to Martin. "She thinks that maybe your dad moving to Alaska had something to do with you and Barney splitting up. What do you think?"

"I think you're nuts," Martin said. He turned to Barney. "I don't think Barney ever liked me anyway." He suddenly pictured Barney on the ice, saying, "It's not my fault. You should have been more careful." Martin's nostrils flared.

Barney's face flushed, thawing. "You never wanted to do anything after he left," Barney said, "except sit around and mope."

"You always thought you were so cool," Martin returned hotly. "Always ordering me around." His eyes narrowed as he stared at Barney. "I think the only reason you hung out with me is because you liked my dad better than your own dad."

Barney opened his mouth to say something, choked, and started to cough. Mr. Raven half stood as he reached over the table and patted Barney on the back.

"What?" Barney wheezed. Mr. Raven sat down.

"You turkey!" Barney's voice was stronger now. "You . . . you *creep!*"

Martin's eyes flashed. "Dad always liked you better. If he could've chosen between you and me to have for a son he'd have chosen you!" Martin heard somebody shouting. He realized that person was him. He clamped his mouth shut. But his anger was suffocating and when he opened his mouth to gulp air, hot, angry words boiled out.

"You and Dad always came up with the neat ideas. *You* always decided when to go camping. Whenever I wanted to, Dad was too busy. *You* were always better at fishing. *You* always got his jokes. And he *always* laughed at your stupid jokes. He *never* laughed at mine."

Martin felt tears creasing his cheeks. One fell off his chin and plopped onto his tray. Barney blurred as Martin blinked. "When he left, you never came around! When he left you never thought about me!" Martin was sobbing. "You *never* liked me!" He looked at Barney and felt a biting cold seize him inside, like the time he'd fallen through the ice. "You're nothing but a turkey with . . . with worm breath!"

Mr. Raven stood up and went to Martin. He knelt and put his arm around Martin's shaking shoulders. "That's OK, Martin," he said softly.

"Get away from me!" Martin shouted. He shrugged off Mr. Raven's arm and pushed his chair away from the table with a loud scraping. "All you care about is my mother! You don't care about me!" Martin stood up and the chair fell backward to the floor with a crash. "If you didn't have the hots for my mom you wouldn't care!" Martin angrily brushed tears away from his face with the back of his hand. Realizing what he'd just said, Martin turned and ran out the door and down the hall. Mr. Raven heard the bathroom door bang as Martin bumped it open and the gentle swoosh as it closed.

Mr. Raven sat down. "Well," he sighed. He looked over at Barney. "Well." Barney's mouth hung open below his startled eyes. "I think that Martin has needed to say those things for a long time."

Barney closed his mouth and nodded.

"How about a cookie for you — and one for Mickey too?" Mr. Raven asked, taking a sandwich bag of cookies from his lunch sack.

* * *

Martin was in a storm of anger and confusion for the rest of the afternoon — feeling like a raindrop caught in the powerful winds of a towering thundercloud, rising and falling, cooling and heating, getting bigger and bigger until he felt so swelled that the currents lost their grip and he fell, like a water balloon, to the ground. When the last bell of the day rang, Martin sprinted outside, not toward home but toward the woods and the fort he and Barney had built. All the war games that he and Barney had played seemed stupid now. Childish. But the fort felt like the safest, most private place to be.

Some of the fort had fallen into the foxhole they had dug under the fort. But the main posts were standing and two sticks they had used for cross beams still straddled the posts. A squirrel was balanced on one.

"Shoo," Martin hissed, and the squirrel scampered to the nearest tree, scolding. "Aw, shut up," Martin barked.

The foxhole was filled with leaves. Martin crawled under one of the cross beams and started tossing out leaves. The leaves on top were crunchy and dry; farther down they were soggy and dank. He scooped his way to the bottom, tossing the debris furiously.

His head bobbed up as he heaved another handful of dirt and leaves and Martin was startled to see Barney, leaning on a large elm tree just outside throwing range, his hands in the pockets of his jeans. Martin stood and his head popped above the fort's cross beams. The small of his back ached where he'd bent up and down, up and down.

"What are you doing here?" His voice squeaked tightly.

"What are *you* doing here?" Barney asked.

Martin wiped his dirt-crusted hands on the hips of his pants. He didn't say anything.

Barney looked down at his sneakers. "Need some help?"

"No," Martin said. He bent down and threw dirt twice as fast as before.

"Hey, Martin?" Barney asked shyly.

Martin continued to throw dirt and leaves out of the fort. He didn't care where it all landed.

"I'm sorry about your dad," Barney said.

"Yeah, I bet," Martin muttered.

"I mean it." Barney straightened and jammed his hands deeper into his pockets. His neck disappeared.

"Well, I'm not," Martin said. "He's a creep."

Barney looked at his feet and pressed his lips together. "You know . . ." Barney took a step toward Martin. He kept looking at his feet.

I wish you'd leave, Martin thought, bending for more dirt.

"You know," Barney said again, "I wish we were still friends." His voice shrank with each word, like a worm retreating into its hole.

Martin stood. He stared, not sure he'd heard right. He hated Barney for being the kind of boy that his father liked and appreciated and understood. Until today, at the business lunch, Martin had never realized how . . . how *jealous* he was of Barney.

And until now, he'd never realized how much he wanted to be Barney's friend.

Martin swallowed and nodded. Barney walked to the fort and sat down opposite Martin. He dug his heels into the wall of the foxhole and watched the dirt crumble into the hole.

"Remember the time we ran away from home and came here to live?" Barney asked quietly.

"Yeah." Martin leaned against the side of the fort. "Yeah, you brought a pack of cigarettes you stole from Clyde's dad and we thought maybe we could live on berries while we made spears to kill squirrels."

"But we got pretty hungry." Barney dug a heel deeper into the foxhole wall. "And then it started to rain."

Martin felt a laugh bubble up from his gut like a burp. "Did your dad whip you when you got home?"

"Yep."

Martin laughed. "Mine too. And he told me the next time I ran away I didn't need to come back."

A shy silence was interrupted by a scolding blue jay. "You know," Barney said, "Mr. Raven's not so bad. But," he added hastily, "I'd sure hate to have him for a father."

Martin looked down at his feet.

"If Mr. Raven and your mom ever decide to get married, you can come live with me," Barney said quietly.

Martin grimaced. "Why would I want to do that, worm breath?"

Barney's face clouded over and, for a moment, Martin was afraid he'd blown it. "Ah, you," Barney sighed, picking up a clod of dirt and chucking it at Martin. "Worms aren't so bad."

They grinned at each other as the tired sun sank into the leafy branches of the trees.

# Chapter 12

"I don't know why we had to invite *them*," Martin whispered to Barney as they waded through the ankle-deep water of Onion Creek. The water was so cold that Martin's toes dug into the squishy insoles of his sneakers, making wet kissing noises with each step.

They hurried along, careful not to splash the water bubbling toward them and not to stumble on the creek's rocks, rounded and smoothed and slippery.

"Without them we couldn't pretend that we're escaping from East Germany," Barney whispered back. "Besides, we've hardly seen them at all."

That's true, Martin thought. But Martin didn't like Clyde or Harold.

"Hey, look!" Barney pointed ahead.

Martin peered into the dappled water, with shadows and puddles of light — khaki and brown and silver — floating into and out of each other. Suddenly his eyes caught a flash of black, like an unfolded pocketknife cutting through the water — a fish, almost as long as his foot.

Martin stopped. Water piled against his ankles. Sand shifted under his right foot and he steadied himself on Barney's shoulder.

"I think it's hiding behind that rock," Martin whispered. His father told him once that fish heard sounds coming from above the water.

"Think we can catch it?" Barney's soft voice sounded as if it were coming from under the stream's burbling water.

"Sure." Gripping Barney's shoulder more tightly, Martin slowly raised one foot, dripping, above the water. He slowly eased it into the water a little closer to the rock and let it sink. When he felt the creek bed, his calf was submerged and aching with cold.

Martin let go of Barney and, slowly, his left foot joined his right foot. Martin stared at the rock as he bent over and slipped his fingers into the water. It's hiding in the shadows, he thought. If I'm careful, it will think I'm a shadow.

Martin's fingers were numb with cold. He held his breath and moved as slowly as a cloud shadow toward the rock.

"Gotcha!" With a loud crash and a whoop Clyde and Harold leaped into the creek from the opposite bank, landing with a splash right next to Barney.

"Whaaa . . ." Barney gasped, jerking his head around. He stumbled and fell into Martin, who splashed face-first into the creek. Just before he hit the water, Martin saw the fish dart upstream and disappear behind another large rock.

Martin scrambled to his feet. "Why, you little buzzards!" He sputtered from the shock of cold water mixed with fear and anger. Harold was standing in the water, dry from the ankles up, smiling, swaying back and forth as if he were drunk. "Hey, Harold!" Martin called, pushing wet hair out of his eyes.

"Yeah?"

"Your pants are on fire!" Martin scooped water into his cupped hands and threw it at Harold. He watched the water stain Harold's clothes and run, like dark paint, down his shirt and shorts.

"Hey!" Harold yelled. "Whad'ya go and do that for?"

"Go soak your head!" Martin yelled back, throwing more water on Harold.

"Watch out!" Barney's warning was too late. Before he knew it, Martin was underwater with Clyde sitting on top, holding his head down.

Barney sloshed over to Clyde, grabbed the collar on Clyde's shirt, and yanked. "Lay off," he grunted. Clyde's shirt ripped and Barney fell backward, sitting with a splash.

"Hey!" Clyde squealed. "My shirt!" He scrambled off Martin, who reared up, sputtering.

"You almost drowned me!" Martin roared. "You bottle thief!"

Clyde's mouth dropped. "I didn't —"

"You took it out of Mr. Raven's desk and got Barney in trouble," Martin yelled, water dripping from his hair and down his face like tears.

Barney's chin jutted and his hands became fists. "Yeah?" He waded toward Clyde.

"Leave him alone. Two against one isn't fair," Harold shouted. He jumped toward Barney and Martin leaped onto Clyde, tumbling into the water. "You lily-livered bottle thief!" Martin bellowed.

Water flew as Barney and Harold and Martin and Clyde wrestled, swearing and tearing at one another's clothes. But, within five minutes, all the anger and fight had washed downstream. They sat in the creek facing one another, panting as if they'd just barely outswum a shark. Clyde sat in his underwear and shoes. His shorts rippled in the current around one ankle like a flag. Harold's shirt hung from one shoulder and he was missing a sneaker, which had floated downstream and was hung up in some branches damming the creek. Martin was missing some buttons, both of his knees were scraped, and his nose was bleeding. Barney had ripped the seat of his shorts and underwear on a branch that stuck out of the bank.

Martin began to laugh first, wiping blood from his nose and upper lip onto the back of his hand. He swished off the blood in the stream. Everybody looked as funny as a wet cat. Clyde began laughing too. Soon all four boys were howling, Barney so hard that he lay down on his back in the water and kicked up his legs, splashing all of them.

"If this fight . . . had lasted . . . any longer," Barney gasped, sitting up, "Clyde . . . would have had . . . to walk home . . . naked! Serve him right, too."

Everybody but Clyde collapsed, laughing harder than before.

* * *

On the way home, Martin's lips were purple and he was shivering violently. The sun retreated under a bank of dark clouds and a breeze kicked up, making goose bumps so hard they hurt to touch.

"Why d-d-d-don't you come ov-v-ver t-t-to my house and-d-d we can ma-ma-make something hot t-t-to drink?" Martin stammered.

"Sh-sh-sh-sure." Barney wrestled the word out. His whole body ached like his head did when he ate ice cream too fast.

They stumbled along, Martin holding himself together with a bear hug, and turned up the driveway of Martin's house. The wind picked up and big drops began to splat onto the pavement. The driveway quickly darkened. Lightning crackled and thunder rumbled deeply.

Martin and Barney stumbled up the kitchen steps. Martin felt as creaky as the screen door, which grated on its rusty hinges as he opened it.

Martin heard him before he saw him. Mr. Raven was laughing nervously, and Franny was saying, "If you don't hold still I'll miss completely."

"Oh!" Mr. Raven exclaimed, sucking in the word. "That wasn't so bad now. But I think you should go in straighter next time."

"Is-s-s that Mr. Rav-v-ven?" Barney's teeth chattered.

Martin nodded, grimly. Why can't he leave us alone? he wondered. Since the business lunch, Martin had avoided Mr. Raven. He'd said things that he didn't want to admit to himself, much less say to Mr. Raven. It made him feel embarrassed and angry, like having someone walk into the bathroom while he was sitting on the toilet.

But Mr. Raven was hanging around their house a lot lately. A couple of evenings a week he would drop by while on his evening walk. Martin usually went to his room and closed the door. He didn't want Mr. Raven to see him watching TV instead of doing his homework. Often, Mr. Raven stayed so late that Martin's mother would drive him home. The five-minute ride sometimes lasted close to an hour.

"Hello?" Mr. Raven called from the dining room. "Hello? Is anybody there?"

Martin silently walked to the stove and turned on the burner under the kettle.

"Hello?" Mr. Raven walked into the kitchen, rubbing the bicep of one arm. "Oh, hi, Martin, Barney. Thought I heard someone come in." He smiled.

"Uh, hi, Mr. Raven," Barney said.

"Want coffee or tea?" Martin asked Barney, ignoring Mr. Raven.

"Tea," Barney answered. "My mom would kill me if I had coffee."

"What in the world happened to you?" Mr. Raven asked.

Martin shook. The ragged tears in his jeans rubbed at his scraped knees. "Nothing," Martin muttered. Lightning popped like a camera's flash.

"Wow!" Barney jumped. The thunder crashed like two planes colliding head-on. Rain pounded like falling debris.

Mr. Raven looked from Martin to Barney. "Why don't you fellas go change into something dry? I bet Martin has something you could wear, Barney. I'll heat the water." He moved toward the stove.

"Where's Mom?" Martin didn't budge, bracing his feet in case Mr. Raven tried to push him to one side.

"She made a quick trip to the grocery store," Mr. Raven said, "and asked me to keep an eye on Franny. Now, Martin, go on and change." He put his hand on Martin's shoulder, pressing the wet shirt against Martin's skin. Martin shivered tensely.

"Hey, what's going on in here?"

Franny stood in the doorway, a syringe in one hand pointed up and her thumb on the pulled-out plunger. "I'm all set," she said to Mr. Raven. She turned to Barney. Her lips stretched into a smile. "What happened to your shorts, Barney?" she asked. "I can see your rear end!" Snickering, she turned and walked back into the dining room.

Barney reached back with one hand and pulled the flaps of his ripped shorts together.

Why is Franny practicing on *him?* Martin fumed. I told Franny I'd let her practice on me. She just never asked. She forgot all about my promise. And Mr. Raven stepped right in and took my place. Just like he's trying to take Dad's place.

Martin heard water rumble in the tea kettle. The rumbling stopped as the water broke into a boil and a cloud of steam billowed from the lid as the kettle began to whistle. Martin shivered. The warm place where Mr. Raven's hand lay on his shoulder made the rest of his body feel colder.

"Mr. Ra-a-ven!" Franny called from the dining room.

"Just a minute, Franny," Mr. Raven answered. Gripping Martin's shoulder tighter, Mr. Raven gently pushed Martin to one side. "Martin, you're shivering. Now go get changed." His voice was firm.

"No!" Martin said, gritting his teeth to keep from shaking. He leaned into Mr. Raven's arm to regain his place in front of the stove. "Leave me alone!"

"Hell-oh-oh!" a voice sang.

Startled, both Martin and Mr. Raven turned to the kitchen door as Mrs. Enders staggered in, clutching a soggy grocery sack that was splitting down one side. Barney let go of the seat of his shorts and reached out to help her set the sack on a counter. "Thanks," Mrs. Enders sighed. "It began to pour buckets as soon as I left the store. Hi, Martin." She glanced at him and did a double take. Her smile dissolved. "Goodness, you look awful. What happened?" She took off her raincoat and draped it over the back of a chair.

"Nothing," Martin mumbled, reaching up to the cupboard next to the stove and pulling out two mugs and then a box of tea bags.

"You better get changed into something dry," Mrs. Enders said. She turned to Barney. "You too."

"We're all right," Martin said, pouring water in the mugs and dunking a tea bag in and out of the hot water in one of the mugs. The water stained as dark as his thoughts. Martin's chin jutted and he tensed his body to keep from shivering. But his shivers built like bubbles in a shaken-up bottle of soda and finally exploded into a shudder so violent that Martin closed his eyes.

"Martin, go to your room. Now! I don't want you to catch your death of cold."

"I agree," Mr. Raven said in his teacher voice. "The tea will still be hot when you two get back."

"No!" Martin said loudly. How dare Mr. Raven act like a teacher here, in *my* house! Martin thought angrily. He picked up the mugs and braced his elbows against his ribs to keep from sloshing tea over the mug rims. He turned from the stove and stepped toward Barney and the small kitchen table.

"Martin." Mrs. Enders's voice was taking on an edge, like a knife being sharpened. "I don't want to argue with you."

Anger and cold grabbed at his insides, kinking his gut, twitching his leg muscles, shaking his knees, and quivering his lips. "I told you, we're OK." His voice was loud and dark. Tea sloshed like a stormy sea and broke over the mug rims like waves breaking on shore.

"Martin!" His mother reached out to rescue the tottering mugs. Martin pulled away. He jumped as hot tea hit him in the chest and then spread soothingly down his shirt.

"Here, let me help," said Mr. Raven, stepping toward Martin.

"No!" Martin yelled, taking another determined step toward Barney, whose head was bobbing between Martin and his mother as if he were watching a tennis match.

"Let's get changed," Barney said quietly. He moved toward the dining-room door.

"No!" Martin bristled like a porcupine surrounded by wolves. He glared at Barney. Whose side
are you on, anyway? he silently asked his friend.

Mr. Raven firmly grasped one of the mugs. Martin
looked up into his smiling face. Buzzard! he thought.
Why don't you leave us alone. Martin jerked the mug
away, and hot tea arced through the tenseness, hung
for a moment, and splattered onto his mother.

"Martin!" she gasped, recoiling and looking down
at the stripe of tea on her blouse. "Go to your room
this instant! I will *not* have you acting this way!"

"Here," Mr. Raven said, reaching for the mug.
"I'll take that." His voice was firm and tight.

"Leave us alone!" Martin yelled, turning toward
Mr. Raven. "Just leave our family alone!" He let go
of the mug, which slipped through Mr. Raven's hands
and fell to the floor. Tea splashed and the mug's handle
snapped, skidding across the floor.

Looking at the mug in his other hand, Martin felt
tears welling.

"Martin, I'm ashamed of you." Martin heard his
mother's voice, muddy with anger, break with frustration.

Martin's chin quivered and tears spilled onto his
cheeks as he looked at her. Swallowing a sob, Martin
dropped the other mug onto the floor, spun around,
and stumbled blindly toward the kitchen door. He
lunged past his sister, who was standing just inside
the dining room.

"Mar-tin," he heard her whine as he lurched toward his bedroom.

* * *

"Creep!" Franny said through her teeth, bursting into their room.

Martin was lying on his back in bed, looking at the ceiling. The light fixture in the middle of the ceiling had collected dead bugs. They were arranged around the buttonlike center hardware in a shape that reminded Martin of Antarctica, viewed from the underside of the globe they had in the school library.

I might as well be in Antarctica, he thought, shivering. He had taken off his wet clothes, all but his underwear, which clutched at him with clammy tightness. He felt a little warmer, but not much.

Martin turned from the fixture to look at Franny. The brightness of the light had seared a bright spot in his vision where her head should be. The rest of Franny, from the neck down, was angry and tense as she jerked books from her desk.

"I hope you're satisfied," she hissed. And her body turned, headless, and left the room. She didn't close the door.

Was he satisfied? Martin closed his eyes. No. He hated the way he felt and acted. Sometimes he didn't know who it was inside of him that hurt people he cared about — his mother, Franny, even Barney. And he hated not being able to control his feelings, especially his anger or his tears. They seemed to take over his body, making him do things that he felt ashamed about.

I really lost control in the kitchen, he thought. I really blew it. He didn't like crying, especially in front

of Barney and Mr. Raven. That was the second time
in two weeks they'd seen him cry. They must really
think I'm a moron, he thought.

Martin closed his eyes. Why do I always come
out looking like a moron? he asked himself. Why can't
somebody like Mr. Raven look bad once in a while?

He heard footsteps coming down the hall toward
his bedroom. He opened his eyes, turned his head,
and saw his mother standing in the doorway, wearing
a clean blouse. "Martin," she said quietly. Her eyes
were angry but her voice and face were calm. "If your
father were here . . ." she began. She closed her mouth
and took a deep breath. Starting over again, she said,
"Martin, we'll be out for a while — Mr. Raven and I.
We're giving Barney a ride home, and then we have
a lot of things to talk about. You and Franny will get
your own supper. I want you in bed by nine. Ten at
the latest."

As she looked at Martin, the anger in her eyes
dissolved into hurt and confusion. "Whether you like
it or not, Mr. Raven is a part of our lives now. Sometimes," she said, her voice suddenly sounding like a
little girl's, "I don't know what to do with you." Biting
her lower lip, she turned and walked down the hall.

Martin stared at the empty doorway. He'd expected his mother to yell at him, punish him for what
he'd done. She should have grounded me, he thought.
Instead she left me feeling more miserable than ever.

Martin listened to the kitchen door close and the
car start. He listened as it faded and was replaced by
the sound of the TV. Martin looked at Franny's side

of their room and felt tired — tired of fighting, tired
of people not understanding him, tired of not liking
himself, tired of not understanding himself, tired of
everything.

Martin got up from the bed, took off his damp
underwear, and walked to his dresser.

"Dinner's almost ready."

Surprised, Martin turned to the door, covering
his crotch with his hands. "Why don't you ever knock?"
Franny stared at him coldly, letting her eyes sweep
up and down his body. "Why can't I have any privacy?"
His voice was pleading. He blushed and wondered if
the rest of him was blushing too.

"You have nothing to hide," she said. "You're just
a kid."

"Then why don't you dress in here anymore?"
Martin asked, turning back to the dresser so he could
uncover himself and reach for his underwear. "Why
do you always go into the bathroom to dress?"

"Because . . ."

Martin quickly stepped into the shorts and yanked
them up. He turned to face Franny.

"Because . . . because I'm not a kid anymore."
And then, for the first time in his life, Martin saw
Franny blush.

"What the hell does that mean?" he asked angrily.
Maybe more than her breasts are developing, he
thought. Maybe she's got hair now. Maybe she's started
to have her period.

"You know," Franny said, "I just don't think that
it would be good for you, that's all."

"You don't think it would be good for me to see

you naked," Martin began, his voice getting louder with each word, "but you think it's OK for you to see me naked?"

"No, stupid," Franny said, standing as tall as she could. "You're still just a boy. I *don't* think you'd understand." She turned and walked back down the hall.

Well, Martin thought grimly, walking to their closet and taking out a shirt and another pair of jeans. Well, well, well. We'll see who understands and who doesn't.

I'm not sharing this room anymore, Martin thought, walking to the hallway linen closet. I'm going to do what Dad never did. He took out a large blanket. Dragging it behind him, he walked back to their bedroom and dropped it on the floor.

"Dinner's ready," Franny said coolly, turning from the stove as Martin walked into the kitchen.

"I'm not hungry," Martin said, pulling open the "junk" drawer. He grabbed a hammer and rummaged around for some nails.

"What are you doing?" Franny asked.

"None of your business," Martin said, leaving the drawer open. He marched back to their bedroom.

He piled books on top of the seat of his desk chair, then climbed up and nailed a corner of the blanket to the ceiling. The blanket hung a foot or so from the floor. That's all right, Martin thought. I don't care if she sees my feet.

Franny ran down the hall.

"What in the world are you doing?" she demanded, standing in the doorway, her hands on her hips.

"I'm sick and tired of sharing this room with you."

Martin got down from the chair, moved it a couple of feet closer to the window, and climbed back on it.

"Are you crazy?" Franny sounded panicked. "After what you did to Mom, you're going to do *this?*" Her voice cracked on the last word. Martin didn't care that she was about to cry.

Martin missed the nail and made a half-moon dent in the ceiling.

"Look, Martin," Franny pleaded. "I'll leave you alone. I'll knock before I come in. I'll knock even if the door's open." Her voice was thick with tears. "I'll move *out. Just don't do this.* Please!" She moved toward the blanket and took hold of it. "Please?"

"Leave that alone," Martin said. He got down and moved the chair to the window.

"Martin!" Franny whined. "*Please!* Don't do this! I don't want to see Mom hurt again. Please!" she panted.

"No," Martin said. He felt rotten but he didn't care. He climbed down from the chair and looked at the blanket. There, he thought. I have my own room.

"You're a *beast!*" Franny cried. "I hate you! I HATE YOU!" She yanked at the blanket, popping out the first nail. It clattered to the floor.

Martin moved toward her. "Don't do that . . ." he threatened. Then he noticed the hammer in his half-raised hand.

So did Franny. A look of horror spread across her face as she stared at the hammer, poised inches from her face. She looked unbelievingly from the hammer to Martin's face. "You wouldn't!" she whispered, color draining from her face.

"You inconsiderate bastard!" Franny yelled. She spun on her heel and slammed the door behind her.

Martin stood in the middle of his side of the room, staring at the bedroom door. For once he'd won — he'd made Franny cry, he'd gotten his way, he was doing what he wanted. For once. But he didn't feel the way a winner should feel. He felt rotten. Just as rotten as when he lost.

The hammer suddenly felt very heavy. It fell from his hand head-first and hit the floor with a loud thump.

# Chapter 13

The blanket didn't stay up long. Even so, Martin's and Franny's feelings scabbed over crustily, unable to stretch or bend without leaking painful beads of anger or frustration.

Although Antarctica now shone on both sides of the room, the nail holes and hammer dents remained. Martin stared at them, unable to sleep, while Franny slept on the living-room couch.

As he waited for his mother to come home and for Franny to come sleep in her own bed, Martin's head filled with a puslike sadness, as if he'd been crying. Finally, he got up. His arms felt as if he were carrying a bowling ball in each hand and his feet felt as if he were walking in thick mud. He grabbed his spiral-ring notebook and pencil and trudged back to bed. Martin rested his feet on his pillow.

The pencil's eraser was flush with its metal band. Martin stuck the pencil into his mouth and, careful not to wet the eraser with his tongue, bit into the

metal band. He looked at the eraser. It had popped
out enough to use it if he needed to. Martin licked his
lips, tasting metal, and began writing, slowly at first
and then faster and faster.

"Jerk face," he began. "I just wanted you to know
that our family is really falling apart now. Too bad you
aren't here to enjoy it. Your wife is still seeing my
teacher and your daughter is falling in love with him
too and even though I try to warn everybody about
him they don't listen. He drinks sissy beer that has
less calories than piss."

Martin admired that last sentence. It sounded like
his father when he'd had a couple of beers. Martin
concentrated, collecting his thoughts, which were flit-
ting around his head like bats. The pencil twitched in
his hand, as if it wanted to write something on its own.

Martin continued writing: "My teacher Mr. Raven
is a slob. But you are too. You never cleaned or washed
or picked up." Martin's feelings strained at his gut,
like his bladder when it was filled to bursting. If he
tried to hold in his feelings his insides would split.

Where were the words? How could he describe
his feelings? Martin wrote, his pencil bobbing, letting
the words chase each other across the paper, letting
his feelings unravel like a thread from the tangle in
his head and run through his arm and hand and pencil.

"And that's not all. You never cleaned up your
feelings after you got angry." His pencil stitched words
as the needle of his mother's sewing machine stitched
thread. "You were a slob and you left your anger all
over the place smelling as bad as your rotten dirty

socks. Why did you leave?" Martin's heart beat faster and faster. "But why would you care anyway? Go on out there and shoot a bear and pretend it's me."

He signed it: "Your ex-son, Martin Enders the First."

Tired and sad and relieved, Martin fell asleep, his feet on his pillow, the paper by his head, the pencil in his hand.

* * *

Mr. Raven didn't visit for the next few days. And, when he began dropping by again, he left Martin alone.

Martin tried to ignore Mr. Raven. At school, that was difficult. Mr. Raven often hovered over him, persistent as a hummingbird at a feeder, encouraging Martin to "keep up the good work." It seemed to Martin that every time he was completely absorbed in something, Mr. Raven would come quietly from the back of the classroom, startling him with a question or an encouraging pat on the shoulder. When Mr. Raven asked how Martin was doing, Martin would grunt or nod. He avoided saying anything to Mr. Raven unless he had to. And when he had to say something he used words no longer than one syllable.

Ignoring Mr. Raven at home was easier. The only thing that Martin couldn't ignore was Franny practicing her shots on Mr. Raven. She finally learned to give herself shots. Even though he'd hated giving Franny shots, Martin missed the different ways she'd gotten him up in the morning.

Spring was as tiresome as a sniffly cold. The perfect weather of the school week soured each weekend.

Rain dripped from the eaves and the wind blew fitfully. Martin and Barney were as anxious for summer as they would have been for a fever breaking. For several weeks, Martin had been looking forward to finding Indian arrowheads with Barney in an old forgotten field surrounded by the forest north of town.

Martin uncurled himself under the blankets, reaching his toes to the cliff at the end of his mattress. Half asleep, he listened for rain. Martin had gone to bed the night before watching a bank of clouds blot out the stars one by one as it snuck across the nighttime sky. Instead of rain, Martin heard his sister softly breathing, still asleep.

This is too good to be true, Martin thought, grinning. He crept out of bed, took a pillow in one hand, and tiptoed toward Franny, who was curled up on her side facing the wall. Franny sighed and straightened her legs. Martin stopped and held his breath. Franny brought her knees back to her chest and breathed deeply again.

Martin took another step toward her. Martin clutched the pillow to his chest. He froze as Franny's breathing fluttered and her legs unfolded again. He raised the pillow above his head.

Wham! He hit Franny on her hip and she threw up her arms and straightened as a diver would just before hitting the water. She twirled around on her back, eyes wide open. "Whaa . . ." she gasped.

"Gotcha!" Martin laughed, threw the pillow on top of her stomach, and leaped on it. Raising his hands and wriggling his fingers like a pianist ready to attack the keyboard, he tickled Franny's ribs, reaching under her armpits. He tried to avoid her breasts. "Stop," Franny rasped. "Stop! Please! Stop!" She laughed helplessly.

"Stop what?" Martin asked, raising his hands and wiggling his fingers in her face. Franny panted, her eyes laughing and fearful at the same time. "Stop war? 'Fraid I can't," he said, and he hunched his shoulders, running his fingers over her ribs as if he were playing the piano.

Franny kicked and wriggled, but she was weak with laughter and couldn't get free. Tears streamed from the corners of her eyes into her ears. She shook her head to get the tears out. "I can't hear," she panted. "Let me up. Please!"

Martin scrambled off her bed. His pajama bottoms had fallen dangerously low and he pulled the elastic band up to his stomach. "I really got you that time," he said proudly.

Franny nodded meekly. "You wait. I'll get you back."

Martin dressed quickly while Franny lay in bed catching her breath. For the first time in a long time, as he put on his expedition clothes, Martin felt like his old self. He felt happy — happy with the bright sunshine outside, with Franny, with himself, with the world.

Martin sat on the edge of his bed and tied the ratty sneakers he used for wading and hiking.

"Your shirt isn't buttoned right," Franny said.

Martin looked down at his father's work shirt.

Sure enough, he'd mated the top buttonhole with the second button from the top. "Whoops!" he said, unbuttoning and buttoning his shirt, his fingers cramped like a knitter's.

"Is that Dad's shirt?" Franny asked.

Martin looked up. "Not anymore," he said. "There. How do I look?"

"Fine," Franny said, sitting up. "That shirt looks good on you."

Martin smiled and strutted out of the room. Better eat a man-sized breakfast, he thought as he walked toward the kitchen. I don't want to carry a big lunch.

He turned into the living room. The nutty smell of pancakes came from the kitchen. What a day! he beamed. Everything is perfect! Mom's making a hot breakfast, just like Dad used to do every Saturday morning.

"Hi, Mom," he said, bursting into the kitchen like morning sunshine. He stopped.

He stared at Mr. Raven, who was standing at the stove, pouring puddles of batter onto the griddle. Mr. Raven's rumpled shirt was untucked in the back. His hair was uncombed. And he was padding around in his socks.

Martin felt numbness creep through him.

Mr. Raven peered over his shoulder. "Hi, Martin," he croaked. His bleary eyes matched his sleepy voice. "Have a seat and I'll get you some pancakes."

Martin stood, frozen to the floor. *What is Mr. Raven doing here? What is going on?*

And then it struck him like a baseball to the head.

*Mr. Raven spent the night at our house . . . sleeping with Mom?*

"No!" Martin jumped at the sound of his own voice. "You didn't!"

"What?" Mr. Raven shook his head slowly. Martin saw pillow creases on Mr. Raven's cheek. "Try to talk a little softer, Martin," he said. "I've got a tremendous hangover. Last night, your mother and I had a little too much to drink and . . ."

"No!" Martin spun on his heel and ran back to his bedroom. He grabbed the doorjamb to stop himself.

"Franny," he gasped. Franny was pulling a polo shirt over her head. "You'll never guess. Mr. Raven and Mom slept together last night! Here!"

"Oh, come on," Franny said, sitting to pull on her shoes. "I'm not going to fall for that."

"Well, it's true." Martin spat the words. He threw himself across the room, ramming into his desk. He flung papers around and frantically opened drawers. "Here it is." He grabbed a bit of paper and raced out of the room.

*Why pancakes? Did Mom tell him that's what Dad used to do?* Wait until Dad finds out, Martin thought, rushing to the phone in the living room.

Martin dialed. The phone bleated when he hit two keys at once. He dialed again and listened to the ghostly static as the phone rang at the other end. Wait until Dad finds out, Martin thought breathlessly. Wait until Dad finds out.

Martin counted five rings. "Hello?" Martin strained to hear above the static. "Hello?" the voice repeated.

Is that a woman's voice? Martin wondered. The voice
was sleepy and rough. Martin suddenly remembered
that Alaska was three or four or five hours behind —
he could never remember which. The last time he
called Alaska, to wish his father a happy birthday, he'd
called around noon and caught his father in the middle
of taking his morning shower. It must be three or four
in the morning, Martin thought.

"Hello?" The voice was more awake. It *was* a
woman! She cleared her throat.

"May I speak to Mr. Enders?" Martin asked
in a small voice. He hoped that he'd dialed a wrong
number — Hawaii, Hong Kong, anywhere but Alaska.

"Mr. Enders?" The woman sounded confused.
"Oh, Warren. Just a minute, I'll wake him up." Martin
heard muffled sounds in the background and whispers.
"Warren. Warren, wake up. Warren!"

Slowly, Martin pulled the phone from his ear and
laid it in its cradle. My father is sleeping with a woman,
he thought. *My dad is messing around with a total
stranger!* He couldn't believe it. Both of his parents
were messing around! His mother *and* his father!

Martin kicked the stand on which the telephone
sat. Its legs shot out and the telephone fell onto the
carpet with a thud. *What's wrong with the world!*
Martin was furious. *Why are adults as messed up
as kids?* Martin kicked at the phone. The receiver
shot forward and then crawled back on the carpet toward him.

Martin's arms ached and he looked down to his
knotted fists.

Martin turned and saw his mother shuffling sleepily toward the kitchen. "Hi, Martin," she said, yawning.

"Damn you!" Martin yelled, running past her.

He ran into the kitchen and screeched to a halt in front of Mr. Raven, who was lifting a pancake from the griddle onto a plate. Closing his eyes, Martin shrieked, "DAMN YOU!" His throat burned.

Martin spun on his heel, but Mr. Raven grabbed his shoulder. "What did you say?"

Martin shrugged to break away from Mr. Raven's grasp and twirled around. Mr. Raven's face looked terrible — puffy and tired. Gulping air and tasting tears, Martin yelled, "Why don't you stay in your own stinky apartment! Why don't you cook in your own lousy kitchen and sleep in your own lousy bedroom! You couldn't find your bed because of all the dirty clothes? You're a slob!" Martin trembled.

"Now wait a minute." Mr. Raven's eyes widened. He pictured his clothes-strewn bedroom the night his apartment was broken into. Mr. Raven shook his head. The last time he'd felt like this was the morning after that. How does Martin know about my bedroom? he wondered.

"Martin," he began.

"You stink!" Martin yelled. "You stink!" And Martin ran out the back door and down the street.

"You stink!" echoed in Mr. Raven's head. He breathed in and smelled the vague scent of deodorant, which blended with the smell of burning pancakes.

\* \* \*

Martin sat under the canopy of the fort. After school he and Barney had lashed new cross beams against the posts and tied fresh foliage all the way around.

They'd also hidden an old metal lunch box of Barney's in the floor of the fort. In it they'd stored crackers and cookies, matches, bandages, a pocketknife that Martin's father had left behind, and a pack of cigarettes.

I'm never going back, Martin thought. He was glad that he and Barney had thought of leaving some things in the fort. I'll eat the crackers and cookies until I rig up a rabbit trap.

I can survive in the wilderness, Martin thought grimly. When Barney comes, I'll tell him to bring some more food and some clothes and a sleeping bag.

Martin's stomach growled. It's time for breakfast, Martin thought, brushing off the dirt that hid the lunch box. He lifted the lid and took out the crackers.

The crackers were dry as cardboard, and he could barely swallow because cracker paste stuck to the roof of his mouth in globs. We should have stored something to drink, Martin thought. He heard water burbling close by, in Onion Creek. But he didn't want to drink any of it without first treating it. Most of the time the water looked clean. But in late summer, when it shrank to a meandering trickle, the creek smelled like the stockyard that drained into it a couple of miles upstream. Air bubbled up from the river bottom like farts in a bathtub of dirty water. When he waded in the late-summer water, his skin felt coated with a sticky, itchy film. He imagined germs squirming on him like kids swarming on a playground.

Barney will have to bring some tablets that'll purify the water, Martin thought, and something to store water in.

Martin sat thinking dark thoughts while swatting the first mosquitoes of the year. He reached into the lunch box and took out the pack of cigarettes. Somebody told him once that cigarette smoke kept away mosquitoes. Besides, he was dying to try one. He lit one and sucked smoke into his mouth until he thought he felt smoke in his ears. He breathed out through puckered lips, aiming smoke as if he were a big aerosol can spraying repellent. He did this several times, getting smoke up his nose and coughing only once. The mosquitoes continued buzzing around his ears and drilling into his arms, looking like bobbing oil rigs with wings.

Barney should bring insect repellent, Martin thought, feeling light-headed. He snubbed out the cigarette on the side of the fort. The roof of his mouth felt as if it were coated with tar paper. I should tell him where my money is hidden so he can buy some things. Or he can ask Franny. She probably knows.

I never want to see anybody again, Martin thought, getting up. He stooped to avoid punching a hole through the fort's ceiling.

In the early morning light, the forest looked watery green. Martin imagined himself standing on the bottom of a pond, surrounded by undulating plants floating to the water's sparkling surface. Everything was blurry. Maybe I need glasses, Martin thought. Or goggles.

*Why is everybody so selfish? Especially my mother?*

Hands in his pockets, he walked toward the creek. *All she thinks about is herself.* Living in Clifton was more important than going to Alaska with my father. Her job is more important than Franny and me. Mr. Raven is more important than we are. *All she thinks about is herself.* Martin scowled at his feet.

If she made a mistake marrying Dad then maybe she made a mistake having me and Franny. Maybe she'd rather not have us at all — get rid of us like she got rid of Dad.

I'll leave her first, Martin thought. I'll never go back home.

Martin stood on the bank of the creek, gazing down. The water was in shadow, looking cold and deep. He gazed upstream, where the bank was less high and the creek was bathed in sun. The water glinted like glassy shards alongside a road.

A little farther up the stream, Martin recognized the place where he fell in through the ice when he skated with Barney. He remembered the cold, as shocking as Mr. Raven in the kitchen that morning. He remembered the anger he'd felt toward the world, the frustration and the hatred. And Barney had been there. He'd lashed out at Barney.

Ever since then he'd felt as though he'd been skating on thin ice. Just when he thought he had his balance and that the ice could support his weight, he would fall through again. And whenever he fell through, like this morning, he froze up inside.

Martin looked up at the trees on the opposite bank. *I wonder if I'll ever get used to everything,* he thought. A grackle cawed and ruffled its feathers. The first line of his report popped into his head: "Any of several heavy-billed, dark birds, larger than crows, of the genus *Corvus*, species *corax*, family Corvidae." The grackle cawed again, flapped its wings, and flew to a tree farther from the creek. Mr. Raven, Martin thought, staring at the grackle, smaller now, its caws less brassy. He shuddered, drawing his father's shirt closer to him and hugging his arms to his chest. It's Mr. Raven spying on me, he thought, shuddering again.

Martin scrambled down the bank. Dirt fell into the backs and sides of his sneakers. He wished that he'd worn socks. Stepping carefully and balancing, Martin crossed the creek on the backs of rocks hunched above the water. He leaped from the last rock onto the sand of the beachlike bank. If Franny wants to, Martin thought, I'll let Barney bring her to visit — if she promises not to tell anybody where I am. Poor Franny, Martin thought. She could never run away and live in the woods. She'd die without insulin. Without regular meals. And, Martin kicked a pebble, they don't deliver the morning paper out here.

He breathed deeply. The air by the rain-swollen creek smelled as if the creek had washed it. The water fizzed like carbonated water, tumbling over rocks in rapids and waterfalls.

Martin walked through the forest, stepping over logs and wiping spider webs off his face. Franny will get along fine with Mr. Raven and Mom, Martin thought. They like her and she likes them.

And they probably won't miss me at all, he thought, feeling as if he'd been hit in the stomach.

# Chapter 14

————+  +————

Barney was waiting for Martin back at the fort, resting against a dirt wall, frowning down at a stick he was whittling.

"Hi," Barney said, looking up, his face relaxing. "You're harder to find than Big Foot."

"Yeah, well, sorry I didn't come over this morning," Martin said, ducking and stepping down into the coolness of the pit.

"That's OK." Barney put the stick down and folded up his pocketknife. "I'm starving. Want some lunch?"

Martin's stomach felt as if a hungry cat were pacing around his ribs, ready to rip hunks from his heart and lungs. "Sure," he said.

Barney reached into a dark corner and dragged out a bulging knapsack. "I couldn't decide what to bring," Barney said, grinning, "so I brought a little of everything."

Barney pulled out a large bag of potato chips. Next, a sack of sandwiches made of homemade bread and wrapped in crinkly waxed paper. Next came several apples and some cookies. And last, with a flourish like a waiter presenting a bottle of wine, Barney pulled out a thermos.

"Worm soup," Barney said, grinning.

They ate silently. The food was good, but hurt and anger filled Martin's mouth with a bitter taste. He took a bite of his sandwich and then put it aside. It stuck in his throat, gagging him.

"Are you feeling OK?" Barney asked.

"Yeah." Martin took a couple of potato chips from the bag. "I'm not going back, you know."

"You running away from home?" Barney asked.

"Yeah," Martin said. It sounded childish — "running away from home." But that's what he was doing — for real. School was almost over anyway. And this summer he could learn to survive in the wilderness and store food for the winter.

"Your mom is pretty upset," Barney said, ripping a bite off his sandwich. Martin winced as Barney chewed. I may need that sandwich tomorrow, he thought.

Barney continued talking with his mouth full. "I've never seen her so upset." He swallowed. "She was even going to call the police."

Martin took a couple more potato chips. Their saltiness made his mouth water, slicking his throat when he swallowed. "She won't miss me after a few days," Martin said. Barney took another bite of his sandwich. "Hey, Barney, could we store the rest of your sandwich in case I need it tomorrow?"

Barney's face froze. "Sure," he said, wrapping up

the rest of his sandwich and licking crumbs from his lips.

"I want to start catching rabbits and fish and stuff like that," Martin said apologetically, "but until I get the hang of it, I'll need regular food."

"Sure," Barney repeated. "Here," he said, handing Martin the thermos. "Maybe it'll still be warm tonight." He handed Martin the knapsack. "I'll bring more tomorrow."

I'll hang this in a tree away from the raccoons, Martin thought.

"What do you say we go looking for arrowheads?" Barney grabbed his fold-up army shovel, which was propped up next to where he was sitting. He remembers everything, Martin thought, looking at Barney and the shovel. Just like Dad. Martin felt a pang of jealousy.

"If you're going to eat rabbits and squirrels and fish and stuff, you could use some arrowheads." Barney smiled and Martin smiled back.

The sun beat down hot, as if focused by a magnifying glass. The air grew thick as gravy simmering on a stove. The forgotten field was in the middle of the forest, square-shaped, with a large stump smack in the middle. It looked like an abandoned farm, and kids made up stories about a ghostly tree that grew out of the stump at midnight during a full moon or at Halloween, its gnarled branches heavy with squeaking bats that hung like shriveled, rotting fruit. Up from its roots, some kids said, crawled the ghosts of all the Indians and settlers who had lived or worked in that

field and now fertilized its soil. These ghosts sometimes attacked couples who necked in the field or
high-school students who had wild parties around the
stump.

Scores of bees buzzed among the spring wildflowers, making the meadow hum as if a large power
line ran through it. As Martin and Barney walked to
the far corner of the field, spring grasshoppers jumped
onto and off of their legs, feeling like fingers poking
them.

Barney stomped on the shovel and it bit into the
sod. Martin dropped to his knees and broke apart the
root-clotted soil, releasing the earth's damp perfume.
With his fingers as much as his eyes, Martin looked
for the signs of arrowheads — slivers of stone with
edges like broken glass.

When Barney tired of digging, they traded places.
Slowly, methodically, silently, taking turns at digging,
they excavated a dark scar along the edge of the field
and then widened it going back.

Worms squirmed from lumps of dirt, sometimes
as tangled and thick as the grass roots, some as big as
baby snakes. Instead of arrowheads, they found a piece
of china with a blue curlicue pattern painted on it.

The sun threw longer, deeper shadows across the
field and, as the air cooled, the boys lost steam.

"I don't think we're going to find anything today,"
Barney said, jabbing the shovel upright into the sod
and sinking down into the grass next to Martin.

"Yeah." Martin threw down the clod he was examining. "We got skunked today." His back ached and
he felt dirty and sweaty.

"Skunked, shmunked," Barney said. "It's about time for me to go back home."

"I'll have plenty of time to look for arrowheads," Martin said, picking up a hank of grass and crumbling dirt off the roots with his fingers. "Ouch!" He looked down at the clod. Poking out was the tip of an arrowhead, so thin around the edges that he could see through the smoky obsidian. With his thumbs, he pushed away the dirt and held the arrowhead up to the sky. "Look," he whispered.

"That's a beaut." Barney craned to look.

"Yeah," Martin breathed. He polished it with his thumb.

Barney jumped up and dug frantically. "There gotta be more where that came from," he said excitedly.

But there weren't. Slowing down, like a car out of gas, they finally stopped. The woods were darker now. The sun had crept closer to the treetops.

"I better get home," Barney finally said, rubbing dirt off his shovel with the ham of his hand. He folded up the shovel.

They walked back to the fort without a word. Barney set the shovel upright against a nearby tree. "I'll leave this here." He looked at Martin uncertainly. "Sure you don't want to come back? I mean, you could stay at my house."

Martin shook his head.

"Want me to call and say you're OK?"

"No," Martin said. "They don't care." He drew a line in the ground with his toe. "Think you'll be coming back tomorrow?" he asked.

"Sure," Barney said. "What should I bring? More food?"

"Yeah," Martin said, "and some tablets that purify water and some paper and a pencil and a toothbrush and toothpaste and a sleeping bag and . . ."

"Wait a minute," Barney said, holding up his hand. "You want me to bring you a teddy bear?" He laughed.

Martin looked at his feet and blushed. "If you need to buy anything for me, ask Franny where I keep my money. It's in my sock drawer rolled up in some red socks."

Barney nodded.

"And don't tell them where I am," Martin said, looking up. "I'm not going back."

"Don't worry," Barney said.

Martin reached out his hand. He'd never shaken Barney's hand before, but it seemed like the right thing to do. Man-to-man, like making a deal or giving your word. I guess when you don't go home anymore, that makes you a man, Martin thought.

"Well, good night," Barney said, awkwardly taking Martin's hand. He squeezed and stuck his hands in his pockets.

"Good night," Martin said, watching his friend disappear down the trail.

"Don't let the bedbugs bite." The forest swallowed Barney's voice.

*I'm alone.* Martin sighed. *Alone and away from Mom and Mr. Raven.* Martin stood in the shadows and weakening light.

"I don't care about you," he said out loud. "Leave

me alone." He closed his eyes and pictured his mother standing by his bedroom door. "Whether you like it or not, Mr. Raven is part of our lives now." The words sounded in his head. He opened his eyes and, instead of his mother, he saw a silent, unmoving oak tree, its roots like tentacles holding the earth tightly in its grasp.

"I'll need wood for a fire," he mumbled, and began gathering tinder and wood, piling it near the fort. When the pile was waist-high, Martin made a circle of rocks and laid the tinder and wood inside just the way his father had taught him. Martin fetched the matches from the fort and counted them. Fourteen. That will last awhile — at least until Barney can bring some more, he thought. Striking a match on one of the rocks, Martin sat back on his heels and watched the curling smoke.

He followed the smoke with his eyes as it reached upward. The sun was sinking fast now and the sky was bruising — blacks and blues rimmed with reds and yellows.

The wind kicked up and held its breath. In the silence Martin heard his mother's teary voice in his head. "Sometimes I don't know what to do with you." Martin breathed out sharply and the wind responded with a quick breath of its own.

"What did you say?" he heard Mr. Raven's voice echo in the forest.

"Creep! Creep!" he heard his sister answer in the distance. And then Martin heard nothing.

The silence was slowly broken by the chatter of squirrels and the rustle of leaves. As darkness fell, the forest noises grew louder. "I better get something soft for a bed before it gets too dark," Martin said aloud. He gathered dry leaves and cut branches from bushes covered with soft-looking budding leaves. He arranged all this against a wall in the fort and tested his new bed. The leaves crinkled and the branches were bony. Martin rearranged the pile and tried again. He itched all over, as if little spidery bugs were crawling on him, climbing out of the leaves and scrambling on top of him. Maybe I should sleep on the dirt floor, Martin thought. He eased himself off the pile of leaves and branches. Yeah, he decided, I'll sleep here tonight.

Martin took the knapsack to the fire. He sat watching the flames lick hungrily at the wood. He took out a sandwich and nibbled, listening, peering into the forest.

The forest was as dark as a cave. But, as Martin peered, trees appeared, and logs and bushes of charcoal and gray. He saw something dart among the shadows and his heart quickened and his lip trembled.

Dad would enjoy this, Martin thought. He's probably camping in the woods now, his rifle by his side, drinking whiskey mixed with coffee, listening to the same sounds I am. Dad enjoyed taking me and Barney camping, Martin thought. In the evening, they would sit around the fire and his father would tell stories — stories about escaped convicts and demented bears and trees that moved in the night, trapping people underneath their roots and sucking out their blood. "Beware of trees that turn bright red in the fall!" his father would growl as the story ended.

What a bunch of puppy poop, Martin thought. "Ha!" He tried to laugh out loud but instead a throaty hiccup came from his open mouth and startled him. "Trees don't move," he said, but his voice sounded scared and small.

I've been camping before, Martin thought, clearing the fear from his throat. But I was always with somebody, he admitted. Martin thought about the places he went with Barney that he would never go to by himself — like skating up the creek in the winter. I'd never do that alone because if I broke a leg or anything, Martin thought, I'd freeze to death before anybody found me.

Being with somebody else makes you feel braver, Martin thought, staring at the fire. And it's scary to be alone when you're used to being with somebody. He pictured his mother's face and his head buzzed like two live wires touching as his mother and this thought connected. She must have been afraid when Dad left, he thought — of men breaking in the house or of not making enough money. She must have felt like I feel now, he thought. Maybe Mr. Raven makes her feel less afraid of everything. He tried to remember a time when he'd seen Mr. Raven afraid of anything. He couldn't. And the only time he'd seen his father afraid was the time Franny went into a diabetic coma and then started thrashing around in convulsions. Martin had been afraid too — that Franny was going to split her head open or bite her tongue off . . . or die.

Nothing will happen to me, he thought, staring

at the fire. He picked up a stick and peeled the bark with his fingernails. The fire leaped and danced and a thought crept into his head like a soldier on hands and knees in enemy territory. But what if a prison escapee is walking around in the woods right now? he thought. That's a pretty big if, he thought. Martin shook his head. But if he's here, he'll see my fire or maybe smell the smoke. He'll want to check it out, to see if he can get any food or a knife or something. What if he was in prison for molesting children or murder or rape?

I'm not *that* cold, he thought. I don't need this fire. Martin shivered as he shoved dirt into the fire's edge with his toe. The flames retreated, as if the fire were sinking through ice into water. Martin drew his knees to his chest and hugged them. Bad guys are attracted to campfires. But animals stay away from fire. Take your pick, he told himself grimly — being tortured and murdered by a child molester or being eaten alive by a rabid raccoon.

At breakfast last week Franny had read aloud an editorial in the paper warning about a rabies epidemic. Martin pictured a rabid raccoon snarling, foam oozing from its mouth and flecks of spit on its chest, its eyes glassy and hateful, staring out from a black mask, walking on wobbly but determined legs.

His heart pounded as he glanced at the stooped shadow of the fort. That wouldn't keep anybody or anything out. And when it rains, it'll fill up with water, Martin thought.

Martin shivered. *What if I get bitten by a black*

*widow? What if I get bitten in the night, in my sleep?
What if I cut myself or break my leg? Nobody would
know.*

His skin prickled, as if centipedes were scurrying
up and down his body, under his clothes. The air was
chilly, but Martin sweated, a cold, dewlike sweat, heated
to an uncomfortable stickiness by the fire. A trickle
slid slowly from his armpit down his side like a slug
creeping down his skin. His skin crawled. Martin
scootched closer to the fire and shivered harder.

Martin's mind whirled. *Would anybody care if I
was murdered?* he asked himself. *Even if nothing happens to me, what will Mr. Raven do when I don't turn
up at school on Monday? By then Mom will have called
the police. Maybe the National Guard. Unless I'm
clever, they'll find me,* he thought.

Martin felt something crawling, spiderlike, on his
back. He grabbed a stick and, reaching over his shoulder, pounded the spot. He winced, but the feeling
was gone. *Maybe they'll find my bones, picked clean,
my sneakers chewed on by some stray dog, my shirt
hanging on a bush, the arms shredded and flapping in
the breeze.*

Martin looked at the sky. The stars, thick and
bright, winked like an army of eyes perched on and
around the treetops. A hoot owl's call sent an avalanche
of shivers down Martin's back.

Spiders and rapists and rabid raccoons and mur-
derers and centipedes and . . . Martin closed his eyes
to stop his whirling thoughts. *Maybe I better go home.*
He opened his eyes and his nerves tingled. Maybe I

better go home. Even living in the same house as Mom and Franny and Mr. Raven is better than being eaten alive.

* * *

Mr. Raven sat at the Enderses' kitchen table and stared at the kitchen window. His face was reflected like a shadow in its silvery darkness and a weak halo shone around his head. The refrigerator began to hum. Mr. Raven looked at his wristwatch. Ten-nineteen.

They've been gone for almost two hours, he thought. I wish Pat would call.

Outside the kitchen door, Mr. Raven heard shoes shuffling on the mat. The screen door creaked. Mr. Raven held his breath and watched the kitchen door open.

Martin stood just inside the door, breathing hard, pale, a thermos tucked under one armpit and a knapsack slung over the opposite shoulder. His hair was tousled and his shirttails were out.

"Hi," Mr. Raven said, trying to hide his surprise.

"Hi," Martin said. He tried to hide his embarrassment, but he blushed.

"You're back," Mr. Raven said quietly.

"Yeah," Martin said.

"Here," Mr. Raven stood up, the chair scraping on the floor. "Let me help." He took the knapsack from Martin's shoulder and, with the other hand, he took the thermos from Martin's armpit.

"Thanks," Martin said, shifting his weight from one foot to the other, looking around the kitchen. "Where are Mom and Franny?" he asked. "In bed?"

Mr. Raven put the knapsack and thermos on the kitchen table and sat down on a chair facing Martin. "They're at the hospital," he said quietly. He reached up his hand and rubbed both of his eyes at the same time. He lowered his hand and looked at Martin. "Franny had a bad spell . . . went into insulin shock. Your mother rushed her to the hospital." Martin's knees felt weak and he tried to swallow the lump in his throat.

"I'm waiting to hear from your mother, to see if Franny's OK. And," Mr. Raven continued, "she'll want to know if you came back . . ."

Mr. Raven pulled the chair next to him out from the table and motioned for Martin to sit. Martin let his legs carry him across the kitchen. He plopped into the chair. *Insulin shock?* Oh, no, Martin thought. His heart hiccupped and his stomach twisted.

The refrigerator stopped humming. Martin stared at Mr. Raven. His hair was uncombed. His eyes were as tired as they had been that morning. Mr. Raven hadn't shaved all day, and his dark stubble was salted with white.

Mr. Raven cleared his throat. "Martin," he said quietly, rubbing his knuckles together. "About this morning." He looked from the window to Martin. "I don't think you understood what was going on."

Mr. Raven saw Martin's body stiffen in his chair. He looked back at his hands. "Last night," Mr. Raven began, "your mother and I had a very serious talk." He grabbed his knees and rubbed his palms harder and harder. "I told her that I wanted to marry her but that I didn't know how it would work out because" —

Mr. Raven looked from his hands to Martin — "because you seem to dislike me so much."

Martin winced. Marriage? As he stared, Mr. Raven nodded. Martin looked at his lap. His ears rang and his jaw clenched. But he wasn't surprised. He knew it would happen all along. He'd known it. And he felt strangely relieved to hear Mr. Raven say it out loud.

"We were at a bar," Mr. Raven continued, "and the more we drank and talked, the more reasons I came up with not to get married." Mr. Raven mechanically ticked them off on his fingers, his voice a monotone. "I'm still getting over the hurt of my first marriage, your mother needs to prove she can make it on her own, I don't make enough money, I haven't known your mother that long, you don't like me, I haven't met your mother's parents, I'm thinking about getting out of teaching and looking for other work."

Tears glistened in Mr. Raven's pinched eyes. Martin squirmed. He'd never seen his father cry, or any other grown man. He felt guilty, as if he was making Mr. Raven cry.

"But your mother told me that she loved me very much," Mr. Raven said, sighing, his smile looking ridiculous. "She said that we all needed more time to get used to such a big change. She thought you were strong enough to understand . . . if we did . . . get married." He looked down again. "She told me that she wanted to talk with you before she said yes, but that she had faith in you — that you'd come through."

Martin's head prickled, as if it had fallen asleep and was just now waking up. His skin crawled as he remembered his fear in the forest. He breathed in, haltingly. He felt safe here with Mr. Raven. His mother felt safe with Mr. Raven. Maybe it wouldn't be so bad. . . .

"But that's beside the point," Mr. Raven said, sighing and sitting up straight. "We drank too much last night. I brought your mother home and we came inside to talk some more and your mother says I fell asleep in the middle of a sentence right on the couch." Mr. Raven smiled sheepishly. "She took off my shoes, got me a pillow and a blanket, and left me there," he said. "When I woke up I thought the least I could do was make a little breakfast. I had no idea you would react the way you did."

Martin sat numbly. He didn't know what to say. So they didn't sleep together, he thought. He'd run away for nothing. Or had he?

"Oh," he said. He felt words crowding in his throat, clamoring to get out, stuck. What can I say? he asked himself.

Mr. Raven nodded, sighed, and looked up at the telephone. "I wish your mother would call," he said.

"How bad was Franny?" The words popped out, tumbling over one another.

"Your mother found her in your bedroom, un-conscious," Mr. Raven said. "Franny spent the whole day running around the neighborhood looking for you. We were so worried about you that we didn't realize she hadn't eaten all day," Mr. Raven said. "And on top of it all she accidently gave herself too much in-sulin."

"Was she in convulsions?""

"Yes," Mr. Raven said, "but your mother got some instant glucose into her and she quieted down. .

"You know, Martin," Mr. Raven said, "I don't seem to bring out the best in you. But I really care about you and Franny and your mother. I want you to know that." His eyes pleaded with Martin and Martin nodded. "And another thing. I'd like you to level with me, Martin. I've been thinking all day — putting two and two together. Did you break into my apartment?"

Startled, Martin looked up. He gulped and opened his mouth. Nothing came out.

"That question is a little unfair," Mr. Raven said. "You don't have to answer. But this morning, you sounded as if you'd been to my apartment and then I remembered about Barney's report and his test both missing."

Martin nodded. "Franny and I just wanted to . . ." A car pulled up into the driveway and its engine sputtered and died. Mr. Raven stood and walked to the door. He opened it and Mrs. Enders and Franny stumbled inside, blinking.

"Martin!" Franny cried. "You're home!" A smile as big as a watermelon wedge broke on her pale face. Martin stood up and Franny threw her arms around him. Martin closed his eyes tight against his tears and smelled the hospital in her hair. He suddenly felt like hugging Franny, but she had his arms pinned to his sides.

Martin opened his eyes and saw his mother. Mr.

Raven was standing next to her, his arm around her shoulder.

Martin's chest heaved, his mouth quivered, and their faces swam as big tears fell onto Franny's shoulder. He gulped a shuddering breath and began to cry harder than he had cried for a long, long time.

# Chapter 15

Martin sat in his bed, a spiral-ring notebook in his lap. *I shouldn't have sent that letter with the shirt.* Martin sighed. I shouldn't have. But I did.

He gazed out the bedroom window. Silhouetted against the low, thick clouds was Mickey's cage, sitting on a nightstand. Breezes puffing into the room brought the faint, sour smell of Mickey's uncleaned cage across the room to Martin. Even though Mickey had died two days before, Martin hadn't cleaned the cage or moved it from its place by the window. The smell and the pee-soaked newspaper were the only things left of Mickey, the only evidence in the world that Mickey had ever been alive. Martin didn't want to clean Mickey off the face of the earth. Not yet anyway.

Martin had found Mickey in the early afternoon, after taking Franny to the airport. The sun was pouring through the window, cooking the damp, yellowed paper in the cage, filling the bedroom with urine fumes. Mickey was slumped over a half-eaten chocolate chip cookie, hugging it tightly — as if he had been afraid the cookie was abandoning him. Or, Martin thought, maybe Mickey just wanted to take the cookie with him to rat heaven.

Mr. Raven didn't know about Mickey yet. Martin decided Mr. Raven had enough to worry about, "tying up loose beginnings," as he had put it, in his old hometown. Besides, Martin dreaded telling Mr. Raven about Mickey's death.

Martin looked at his notebook. Mr. Raven hadn't wanted to visit — back where his ex-wife and her boyfriend lived. When Mr. Raven told Martin, Franny, and Mrs. Enders that his ex-wife had invited him to her wedding, they all decided that Mr. Raven should send a nice gift and not go to the wedding. Franny suggested that Mr. Raven send a gum ball. Martin suggested that somebody chew it first. Mrs. Enders suggested a book on raising babies, so that's what Mr. Raven got. Martin and Franny wrapped it for Mr. Raven and tied it up with a zillion tiny bows. The wrapped gift was beautiful, but it would be extremely difficult to open.

Martin looked out the window. The clouds were moving in like a blanket, tucking themselves over and around the sky, putting the day to sleep.

Martin looked back at his notebook. I shouldn't have sent the letter, he thought. I've never really told Dad what I thought of him before. But two weeks ago his mother told Martin that his dad had asked if Martin and Franny could visit Alaska for several weeks. He even enclosed a check to cover the plane fare.

Franny was overjoyed. "Oh, I wonder if we'll get to see Eskimos," she said, hopping from one foot to the other. "It's supposed to be light up there all day and all night at this time of year! Maybe we'll see some polar bears!"

She raced to their bedroom. Martin followed her, hands in his pockets. He stood at the door, disgusted, watching her pile the clothes on her bed that she wanted to take. Martin decided right then and there not to go.

"I don't want to leave you all by yourself," he told his mother later, "without a man around the house."

"Mr. Raven can help when he comes back . . . if I need help," his mother countered.

Since school had been out, Mr. Raven seemed like a different person — fun, relaxed, understanding. Martin and Barney and Mr. Raven had gone camping last month and, just before he left, Mr. Raven taught Martin how to cook the best spaghetti sauce he'd ever tasted. They'd boiled spaghetti, throwing it against the wall to see if it would stick. If it did, the spaghetti was done. When his mother came into the kitchen to check out the noise, she'd found them leaning against the counters laughing. Mr. Raven had a strand of spaghetti across his hair, like a huge part. And Martin had one wound around his neck.

Every once in a while Mr. Raven sounded like a teacher, but not often. Even so, Martin didn't tell his mother that one reason he didn't want to go to Alaska was that he thought Mr. Raven might help his mother too much. Martin wanted to be sure Mr. Raven didn't move in and make pancakes *every* morning in their kitchen while he and Franny were gone.

Besides, Martin wanted to be home when Barney got back from his vacation in Maine. And Martin was anxious to find another arrowhead in the meantime.

His mother had insisted that he go. "I don't want to go," he finally said. "I don't want to see Dad. Not yet."

His mother threw up her hands and sighed. "All right, Martin. I won't say any more. But I think you're making a mistake. You don't have a chance to go to Alaska every day, you know."

Instead of going, Martin asked Franny to take his father the work shirt Martin had worn so much and hadn't washed. The shirt had smelled like his father when Martin first wore it. Now the shirt smelled like Martin, even in the armpits. He had made his father's work shirt *his* work shirt — its smells were his own and its wrinkles and dirt were his own. He hoped that his father would take the shirt out of its box, smell it, look at it, put it on — and think of Martin the way Martin thought of his dad every time he had worn it.

Martin felt good about sending the shirt. But at the last minute, he added the letter, laying it on top of the buttons of the shirt's front and folding the arms of the shirt over it like a hug.

I shouldn't have done that, Martin thought again. He opened the notebook on his lap. He'd written the letter in his notebook first and then copied it neatly for his father, keeping the rough draft.

"Dear Dad," it began. "How are you? I am fine.

Nothing much is going on. I just wonder what you've been up to and if you've bagged a moose yet."

The blue lines across the paper were almost invisible in the gray, cottony light. Martin continued reading. "Barney and I went camping last month with Mr. Raven, our teacher. At least he was our teacher until school got out. Now he's just Mr. Raven. Anyway, we went to the Ledges and we showed Mr. Raven all the trails you and Barney and me used to hike. He knows almost as many flowers and plants as you but not quite. I used to think he was a terrible teacher but we see him a lot lately. I'll let Mom write you about that.

"Franny's doing OK. But you know that by now. She's giving herself her own shots so you won't have to do it. We read in the paper a while ago how maybe they can do away with insulin shots by planting parts of the pancreas inside people who have diabetes. Franny thinks that's neat. She said that maybe she learned to give herself shots too soon. Ha Ha. I'm glad I don't have to give them to her anymore.

"How is Alaska? Have you made any friends? Barney says hi. Write to us and let us know how you are doing."

Martin's eyes stopped and unfocused and the letters on the page blurred. He wanted to say so much. Like the pencil writing on the paper, he'd only scratched the surface. How can I tell him about Mom and Mr. Raven or Mr. Raven and me or Barney? How can I tell him about running away and about Mickey? Maybe he's not even interested, Martin thought.

Franny better tell me everything when she gets back, he thought, looking at her empty bed. She better tell me if Dad is living with somebody or if he asked about me or if he is happy or misses being with us.

He looked back to the notebook. In the space at the bottom of the page he'd written, small and scrunched: "Martin Enders the First."

Maybe someday I'll visit Dad, Martin thought. Maybe someday I'll be able to tell him some of those things and whatever happens in the meantime. Maybe. But then, Martin thought, closing the notebook and tucking it under his pillows, maybe not.

Printed in the United States
5001

9 780595 200191